MOC

SEA LIGHTNING

Patagonia, literally the ends of the earth, did not sound a likely place to find romance. Nor was it, Jensa soon discovered, when she went there to work for Dr Adam Ryder on his study of whales—and encountered nothing but hostility from him. He definitely preferred whales to human beings—at any rate if the human being was called Jensa Welles! Could she stick it out until her job was completed?

SEA LIGHTNING

BY

LINDA HARREL

MILLS & BOON LIMITED
15–16 BROOK'S MEWS
LONDON W1A 1DR

*First published 1979
Australian copyright 1979
Philippine copyright 1983
This edition 1983*

© Linda Harrel 1979

ISBN 0 263 74267 9

Set in Linotype Plantin 10 on 11½ pt.

01–0383

*Made and printed in Great Britain by
Richard Clay (The Chaucer Press) Ltd,
Bungay, Suffolk*

CHAPTER ONE

JENSA WELLES set her shoulder bag down on the battered wooden bench and, with growing unease, scanned the knots of shouting workers and restless travellers inside the cavernous metal air terminal. Lack of proper sleep, plus jet lag and the weight of her equipment bag—which she had insisted stay with her every moment of the five-thousand-mile journey—had combined to make her dizzy and weak. And, if she were to admit it, a little panicky.

Josh had said she'd be met. But the rest of the passengers on the small Argentinian airliner had long since been greeted and embraced and helped off by assorted relatives and business associates—or, at the very least, an efficient porter.

It wasn't that she had so many bags to see to. Only one, in fact, in addition to her handbag and the hard case containing her supplies. There had simply been no time, after she had accepted this assignment, to assemble much of a wardrobe. It had been a desperate rush to gather the necessary equipment, passport, traveller's cheques.

But the dismal fact was that Jensa, in addition to not speaking a word of Spanish, didn't have the first idea of where to turn for help. She had a name only—Dr Adam Ryder. 'They'll take care of everything at that end, my dear,' Josh had said. 'They'll *have* to,' Jensa had replied, laughing. 'I don't happen to keep a wardrobe suitable for the rigours of a Patagonian winter in my

5

closet—my own winter things are still in the cleaners' storage. And with the temperature in Montreal nudging ninety, I suspect that the stores will have a rather meagre supply of down jackets on their racks!'

She had grinned at Josh, and he had laughed reassuringly. He seemed to have no doubts about her accepting the job in place of himself. He evidently had every confidence in this Dr Ryder. Why shouldn't she?

The hoarse yells of the workers and the crashes of the wooden supply crates as they came hurtling down chutes echoed in the draughty hangar, and Jensa felt a headache tighten its grip about her temples. She felt, too, a prickle of fear flick the nape of her neck.

Annoyed with herself for allowing her emotions to be dictated by a tired body, she reminded herself sharply of the exhilaration she had experienced just a few hours earlier as her taxi had wound its way through the narrow old streets of Buenos Aires. She had been transferring from the main airport and a sleek 747 to another airport and the small plane that would take her to the bustling coastal town of Puerto Madryn.

She had been dazzled by the beauty of Buenos Aires with its mixture of old Spanish charm and modern polish. And she had been very sure, then, that her undeniably impulsive decision to take this assignment had been the right one. It would be a wonderful adventure, and a rare opportunity professionally as well.

But her spirit of adventure was fading very decidedly. The cosmopolitan glamour of Buenos Aires seemed a long way away from the clutter and drabness of this hangar. And instead of a warm welcome from a relieved and grateful Dr Ryder, she was left, instead, feeling increasingly foolish and worried in turns.

She was, she realised uncomfortably, beginning to draw curious stares. And some of the attention would be of the decidedly unwelcome sort. Not that she wasn't accustomed to having people, particularly men, stare at her, but here, in this land of darker skins and raven hair, her pale, almost transparent blonde looks were sure to attract attention.

She was dressed casually for travel in a tailored brown tweed pants suit, high-heeled boots, and a good beige raincoat. But she still managed, with her tall, graceful carriage, to attract. She shifted uncomfortably on the bench as groups of workmen looked, talked among themselves, sometimes laughed.

There was attention from another direction as well, she noticed impatiently. A man, lounging against the ticket counter, talking to the clerk in rapid Spanish, had more than once turned a rather insolent gaze the length of her. He appeared to be waiting for something, a shipment perhaps. The clerk had been putting in calls for him but without, judging from the shrugs, much luck.

Darn! she thought. Where *is* Dr Ryder! What if it were just a horrendous mix-up? It was, after all, still hard for her to believe that she could be in Montreal one day, and a few days later be stuck in a remote airport thousands of miles away.

Her eyes fell again on the man standing at the ticket counter. English, she thought. Somewhere in his thirties. He *could* be the one sent to pick her up. But why hadn't he approached her? That he was acutely aware of her presence she had no doubt.

Furtively, she tried to size him up. She took in the hard set of the stubborn jaw, the aggressive thrust of one hand on his hip. He was an unusually tall man, and well built, she noted unwillingly. His angular features were deeply bronzed from sun and wind, and the thick brown hair, long and shaggy from lack of recent barbering, was streaked from the sun as well.

No, she thought. He couldn't possibly be someone sent by Dr Ryder. More likely a workman from one of the huge ranches to the south than someone who would be acquainted with a brilliant scientist like Dr Ryder. This man was decidedly coarse.

At that moment his eyes rose and met hers. Jensa felt colour come to her cheeks at the slow smile that appeared on his face. She knew that smug and frankly appraising look so well—and detested it. Deliberately, she raised her head a fraction and turned away from him, her eyes cold. But not before she had seen his mocking grin.

She'd have to get a grip on herself, she told herself bracingly, start making sensible enquiries. Perhaps Josh had said something that would help her locate the research station.

Jensa had studied art under Josh Hager for three years. It was he who had seen her talent, believed in her and encouraged her during those bad times when her family had pressured her to give up her ambitions and settle either for marriage or a more 'sensible' career.

Jensa believed she owed it entirely to Josh that she was already so well established as an illustrator. Her delicate drawings of plants and animals and children were now in demand as book illustrations by a small but select international following. And Josh, never known for his modesty, would indeed agree that he had been the key to his former pupil's success. But that soaring talent, he would say, smiling gently, had been there all along.

It was Josh, of course, who had been this Adam Ryder's choice. The famous marine biologist wanted only the best to work on his study of whales, just now drawing to a close at his isolated observatory on the remote, windswept coast of Argentina called Patagonia.

And then there had been the car accident—not desperately serious, but enough to make it impossible for Josh to go. 'There are hardly any people down there, let alone doctors and medical centres,' Josh's wife Evie had wailed the day after the accident. No, it was out of the question, and a cable had been sent to Dr Ryder notifying him of the delay.

The reply had been immediate and emphatic. The whales would be at the breeding grounds for a limited time—it was now or never for the illustrations. Next year there might be no research grants. The breeding grounds themselves were in danger of destruction. The cable pleaded that Josh find a capable substitute.

Jensa had perched on the edge of a chair next to Josh's hospital bed and frowned at the big, bear-like form propped up by a small mountain of pillows. '. . . and you know, Jensa,' he was saying, 'that you're the only illustrator, next to me, who can capture the feeling Adam wants.'

'He's the type, I take it,' said Jensa, 'who knows exactly what he wants.'

'He is,' Josh agreed. 'Adam can be very demanding —we worked together a few summers ago on Vancouver Island when he was doing a study on orcas— killer whales. But you're more than up to it, my dear. I wouldn't throw you to this particular lion if you weren't!'

'*You* may think my work's good enough, Josh, but what about him! If he's as fussy as you say, will he be willing to accept a perfect stranger—without having at least seen some samples?'

'Told you,' said Josh, shaking the broad, bearded head, 'from the point of view of his research, Adam's desperate. Besides, he trusts me. I would never send him anyone who wasn't up to his standards—I respect the work he's doing far too much for that.'

Jensa re-read the cable. ' "Trust your judgment. Timing vital. Payment the same".'

Jensa sat back in the chair and shook the long strands of cornsilk hair. '*I* couldn't accept that kind of fee, Josh! That's for someone of your stature, not someone still relatively unknown.'

Josh looked exasperated. 'You are no such thing,' he said sternly. 'And surely dropping a sane person's life and trotting off to Patagonia on a few hours' notice deserves a pretty generous reward! Besides,' he added, grinning like a mischievous child, 'it's precisely the sort of impulsive, romantic escapade that we artistic types thrive on!'

Jensa's generous mouth curved upwards and returned the smile. She did want the assignment—very much, she realised. Certainly it would be a prestigious item to add to her portfolio. Beyond that, she was between major assignments, and this one would be a welcome change from her last.

She had just wound up a series of illustrations for an article in a medical journal. The drawings were of an operation at a children's hospital to reconstruct the face of a badly burned child. It had been a demanding job, both physically and emotionally, and Jensa had thrown herself into it, determined to do everything she could to help the pathetic little girl.

The operation was a success. But it had left Jensa drained, and she had given herself a week off—to do nothing, she had told everyone, more demanding than file her nails or, at the most, sketch a few squirrels in the park.

And so she had accepted the Ryder assignment.

'Better hop to it, my dear,' Josh had commanded. 'I'll cable Adam that I've found him an admirable replacement and that you'll be arriving using my schedule!'

Jensa planted a kiss on Josh's cheek, then hurried out of the hospital to attend to the multitude of arrangements that would have to be made.

Smiling and shaking his head in a mixture of amusement and affection for his young protegée, Josh lifted the telephone and dialled the telegraph office. 'The cable should read: "Former student Jensa Welles has accepted the position. Highest recommendation. Will arrive per my schedule ..." and sign that Josh, would you please, operator?'

Jensa straightened her shoulders. Something was amiss, and she'd better get on with finding a solution. To her dismay, however, the clerk had vanished into a supply room. The only one who looked remotely as if he might speak English was the man who'd been eyeing her so provocatively. She looked at him again, noting with distaste the mud-caked jeans and the coarse black wool sweater, the sleeves of which were thrust up to expose strongly muscled forearms.

Better than nothing at all, she concluded. But she'd keep it very businesslike—his sort usually didn't need much encouragement. Picking up her few bags, she approached the counter.

'Excuse me. . . .' she began. Startling blue eyes set in bronzed, weathered skin met hers sharply. '. . . excuse

me,' she began again, 'but I wonder if by *any* chance
you'd be the person who was sent to meet me. You
see——'

He cut her off abruptly. 'Sorry,' he said. 'I was supposed to pick someone up from the last flight—but not
you, unfortunately. I was to meet a man.'

Jensa's heart sank, and exhaustion and disappointment combined to erase the air of command she had
attempted to display. Despite an edge of impatience in
his voice, the man looked down at her with something
close to sympathy on his face.

'Perhaps,' he said, 'if you tell me who was supposed
to meet you—I know a few people in Puerto Madryn.'

Jensa brightened. 'Oh, really? He's probably quite
well known around here—his name is Ryder. Dr
Adam Ryder.'

He looked at her without expression for a second,
then said dryly, 'I don't know how well other people
around here know him, but *I* know him quite well——'

'Oh,' she cried, beaming. 'What luck! Could you tell
me where I might find him?'

'You've got him. I'm Adam Ryder.'

Jensa stared at him, astonished at first, and then relieved, her first impressions of this man forgotten altogether. She was not to be stranded in the middle of
nowhere after all! 'I'm Miss Welles,' she said, extend-
ing a hand, 'Josh's replacement.' But his hand did not
come up to take hers, and the eyes that met hers were
utterly hostile.

'I can't think what you're talking about,' he said in
icy tones. 'I came here to meet a man—not you.'

The words were uttered with such distaste that
Jensa's spine stiffened. What on earth was going on
here? Whatever it was, it had better get settled right

now, before she gave way entirely to fatigue and frustration.

She took a deep breath and said with deliberateness, 'There has evidently been some confusion, Dr Ryder. Josh told me that he was going to send you a telegram confirming that I'd accepted the job—did you not receive it?'

'I received it all right—I've got it right here. And it certainly doesn't say anything about a woman.' He reached into the back pocket of his jeans and produced a crumpled piece of paper which he handed—or thrust, rather—at Jensa.

She took it and read it, frowning. Then her eyebrow arched and she laughed.

'You find something funny in that?' he asked in considerable irritation.

For the first time in hours Jensa's smooth cheeks dimpled, and her voice rose almost gaily. 'Well, not funny, perhaps, but a relief, certainly! There, you see? It's just a slip on the part of the telegraph operator.' She turned the cable back to him, pointing. 'She's written "Jens", instead of "Jensa". Maybe because a man phoned it in . . . and you don't hear my name too often, I suppose.'

He stared at the cable for a moment, then turned on her incredulously. 'Then . . . *you're*——'

'That's right. I'm Jensa Welles—with an "a"!' She smiled encouragingly at him.

The response was a single, harsh word. Jensa winced and pulled back as if slapped. His astonished expression had now turned positively glacial. 'What the hell did Josh think he was doing, sending a woman in his place—he must be sicker than I thought!' He slammed a calloused fist on to the counter.

'Well,' he said in low, clipped tones, 'whatever your name is, you can get on the next flight back to Buenos Aires—I'm not taking any woman down to the station!'

Jensa swallowed hard to contain her rising temper. 'Dr Ryder,' she began evenly, 'I saw the cable you sent to Josh. You made it very clear that anyone of whom Josh approved would suit you just fine. You did not specify the sex of the artist!'

'Because it never occurred to me that Josh could be fool enough to send a woman down here. You look frazzled enough already—you wouldn't stand up three days, let alone three weeks, down there.'

Jensa, her anger finally snapping, rapped out, 'Dr Ryder, I've come through two days of travel that would stagger an elephant ... and, yes, I'm tired. But I don't see how that makes me weak or unqualified. I simply need a shower and a decent night's rest and I'll be perfectly fine!'

'Good. And as soon as you make this miraculous recovery you can get yourself on the next flight out of Puerto Madryn back to Montreal!'

'But you haven't even seen my work!' she protested, practically sputtering in frustration. 'I've lugged samples of my books half way around the world. You can't just send me packing without at least seeing what I'm capable of—it's preposterous!'

He loomed over her, his eyes utterly cold and uncompromising. 'Look, Miss Welles, you could be another Michelangelo and I'd still be giving you the boot —that station is simply no place for a woman.'

A change in tack was required, thought Jensa, saying quickly, 'It's very chivalrous of you to be concerned about my welfare, Dr Ryder, but I can assure you that——'

'I don't give a damn about your welfare,' he shot back. 'It's my work I'm concerned with. I will not jeopardise years of study by saddling myself with a woman completely unprepared for our circumstances!'

That does it! she thought. Exhaustion and disbelief at his reception—so different from what she had envisaged—made her lash out without reserve. 'Dr Ryder, you are an arrogant, opinionated chauvinist! What on earth has my sex got to do with illustrating a book?' She could sense the anger in him, coiled as tightly as the muscles in the hands which rested on his hips. But she would not back away from this confrontation.

'We're simply not set up for a woman,' he blazed. 'Did Josh neglect to tell you the conditions under which you'd be working?'

Jensa tilted her head to face this bully squarely. 'He said they'd be rugged—and it made no difference to me. You must have been holed up here in Patagonia for donkey's years, Dr Ryder, that's all I can say! It's been ages since women required—or expected—special treatment. I can survive in exactly the same conditions as you, thank you very much!'

Surprisingly, he seemed to hesitate just a fraction of a second. It was faint encouragement, but Jensa grabbed at it. Perhaps he was capable of listening to reason after all. 'Look,' she pressed on, her voice softening just a little, 'I'm a professional, Dr Ryder. I've come a very long way to do a job, and do it well. I would like you to extend me the courtesy of allowing me to prove that I can do just that. I do not need, nor do I want, to be treated as anything other than a completely equal co-worker.'

She held her breath and waited as the sardonic gaze

travelled the length of her. Lounging back against the counter, he drawled, 'Our project would certainly be a test of anyone's professionalism—man or woman. But since you're so fully professional, I gather you've come prepared. Where are the rest of your bags?'

She hesitated, sensing a trap. 'This is it,' she said.

'I see,' he replied, with an air of tired exasperation. 'And in that little bundle I suppose you've got everything you need to cope with our somewhat changeable climate—plus the rocks and the sand and the ocean.'

'That's a cheap shot, Dr Ryder,' Jensa snapped. 'I had only a few hours to make all the arrangements for getting down here. I do have other obligations, you understand. But I assure you I'm perfectly prepared in terms of art supplies.'

The face that looked back at her wasn't the least bit apologetic, she thought. The man didn't appear to have a single weak spot in him. Being reasonable certainly didn't work. And she couldn't intimidate the likes of this ruffian.

She brushed a strand of hair from a flushed cheek. She'd not turn around and go back to Montreal in defeat. Her instincts told her that outmanoeuvring this man would be nothing short of dangerous. But she'd play her best card—she had to.

'If I understand the situation correctly, Dr Ryder—and I believe I do—my coming here has saved your neck! You need me,' she said triumphantly. 'Where are you going to find another well-qualified specialist who'll drop everything and come to the end of the earth to rescue you and your project?'

She stood back, flushed with anger, delicate nostrils flared, not caring any longer what he said or did. Rude, ungrateful man!

His silence and the clear exasperation told her she had been right—he really did have no choice. It was Jensa, or the project would flounder just at its conclusion.

The broad shoulders shrugged. 'You'll find our selection of clothes here rather limited, Miss Welles, but you should make it through with jeans, workboots, maybe a native poncho for the cool nights.' He bent and picked up her artist's case, and with long, sinewy strides, headed for the door.

So that's to be it, she thought. She supposed she was hired, but he wasn't even going to have the decency to tell her politely. Some month this was going to be! Grabbing her suitcase, she skipped after him.

She was happy, she told herself. So why was a small bell of warning tinkling in her head? 'Nonsense,' she said aloud, and strode ahead to where he stood waiting in a dusty parking lot.

'That's ours,' he said.

'My first encounter with roughing it, I take it,' she replied, eyeing the muddy interior of the Land Rover and the alarming bumps protruding from the well-worn seats.

'That's right,' he said humourlessly, as he tossed her things into the back. 'And you'll find it downright luxurious compared to where we're heading.' Jensa stole a secret glance at the strongly sculptured profile and saw not a hint of mellowing.

There were no sides to the Rover, and she clung to her seat as he started the engine and drove much faster than she thought necessary out of the lot. But he shifted the gears with surprising gentleness, she noted, and slipped skilfully into the heavy flow of traffic.

They rode in silence, Jensa trying to quell the apprehension that gnawed insistently at her stomach, Adam Ryder seemingly intent upon the traffic. The wind lifted the thick brown hair, and exposed clearly the strong, high brow; the grip of the broad, brown hands on the steering wheel told her—if she had ever doubted it—that while he was going to give her a chance, he was not happy.

In the centre of the bustling town, he brought the Rover to an abrupt halt. 'Not a department store by your standards, but I think you can find everything you'll need. Did you bring any working clothes at all?' he asked, switching off the motor and turning to her.

Jensa frowned. 'Well, one pair of slacks . . . a couple of tops, I suppose. . . .'

He cut her off. 'Anything warm—this is winter down here, you know.'

'A sweater—and this raincoat. My winter things were all in storage.'

'O.K., O.K.,' he said impatiently, 'get yourself several pairs of jeans, some warm tops—nothing fancy, heavy sweat-shirts are best. And a native poncho, as I said, would be a good bet. And boots.' He eyed her fine, heeled boots derisively. 'It's rough and rocky climbing around the station.'

'So much for just a few weeks?' Jensa protested. 'I'm sure I could get by with just a fraction——'

'Miss Welles,' he rapped out, 'if you're going to question everything I tell you to do, I can see we're in for a time of it. You're going to be constantly wet and dirty—enough so as to make you thoroughly miserable, if not actually ill. You'll be needing several changes.'

Jensa opened her mouth to apologise, then thought better of it. It would be wasted on him, she thought. She watched as he pulled a wallet from his back pocket and drew several large bills from it. 'This should cover it generously.'

She took the money. Perhaps, she thought quickly, he wasn't such a bad sort after all.

She ventured a conciliatory smile. After all, if he had come prepared for a man, the sight of her must have been a bit of a shock. Now that he had accepted the idea of her, perhaps their bad start could be put behind them. 'This is really terribly kind of you, Dr Ryder,' she said.

'It has nothing to do with kindness, Miss Welles. Without proper equipment you're absolutely useless to me. And I assure you, it will all come out of your pay-cheque.'

With that rebuff, two arms like bands of steel came down over hers, and she was deposited over the side of the Rover like a sack of potatoes. The motor roared to life again.

'I'll pick you up in an hour,' he shouted. 'Don't be late. We're wasting enough time as it is!' Gravel kicked up from under the wheels and he was gone, leaving Jensa alone on the sidewalk, anger and embarrassment colouring her cheeks. Josh, she thought, huffily shoving the strap of her purse over her shoulder, your ears must just about be on fire by now—you've got *two* of us blessing you! And it looks as if that's the only thing Adam Ryder and I will ever agree on!

A cache of crumpled brown paper bags stacked neatly beside her, Jensa stood at the kerbside less than an hour after her unceremonial dumping by her reluctant employer. She had shopped quickly, determined to deny him the opportunity of calling her a typical female given to lengthy shopping sprees. That would certainly be his style!

The narrow old street was clogged with a variety of farm vehicles and transports. The air was thick with exhaust fumes and blast from a horn made Jensa wince. Uneasily, she realised that she was becoming unsteady on her feet. Falling prey to jet lag, she supposed, and craned her neck to see if she could pick out the battered Rover from the armada of vehicles rumbling up the road. A raw winter wind, ocean-scented, made her shaky balance even more uncertain, and she clutched the thin material of her raincoat tightly about her. How long had it been since she had eaten? Hours, she realised.

She was desperately glad to see Adam Ryder when he finally pulled up, although she wondered whether she would be up to going another round with him if he choose to continue his combative manner.

'All done?'

'Yes, thank you,' she replied as crisply as her swimming head would allow. She began heaving the parcels into the back of the Rover. He swung his long body easily over the side, and she said quickly, 'I can manage quite well, thank you, Dr Ryder.'

'Right,' he replied mockingly. 'You're the girl who wants no special favours—but you needn't worry: I intend to offer none. I want to check one of the tyres that was acting funny.' He smiled, but at her expense, she knew. Grimly, she finished wrestling the last parcel into the car.

She had no real warning—she simply fainted. The next thing she knew she was sitting in the front seat, carried there, she supposed miserably, by Dr Ryder. What an infernal nuisance he must think her! Chagrin quickened an already racing pulse.

She blinked rapidly, trying to clear her frustratingly fuzzy thoughts, and for the first time noticed the small crowd of curious onlookers, mostly giggling children, that had gathered round them. Struggling upright, she sputtered an apology.

'Easy now—try that and you'll end up flat on your behind again in front of your audience.' Strong, restraining hands pressed her into the bend of his arm. But she needed no encouragement; even that small movement had set in motion again the sickening swirl in her head. She eased back gratefully and buried her face in his shoulder to escape the painful pinpoints of light that danced before her eyes.

'I know you won't believe this,' she whispered, 'but I usually don't do things like this at all. I'm really disgustingly healthy—I can't think what came over me.'

'I can. You're exhausted and your stomach is empty. We'll stop in somewhere and get you some solid nourishment before we hit the road.'

The thought of food made Jensa's already queasy stomach constrict sickeningly. 'I'm sure I couldn't eat. . . .' she began.

'Arguing again,' he noted, withdrawing his arm from around her and firmly pressing her against the seat. 'You *are* going to curb that tiresome habit, aren't you?'

He took her to a small restaurant in the working section near the docks where he was greeted enthusiastically and by name by the owner. 'Food around here tends to be robust and no-nonsense—but extremely fresh and good. It'll set you up again,' he predicted.

Jensa's violet eyes rolled heavenward at the thought of anything heartier than tea and dry toast, but she knew that nothing in the world could impel her to protest.

The house speciality seemed to be local lamb grilled

over charcoal in the open kitchen. Adam ordered it for both of them. She declined a taste of his appetiser—some kind of raw fish marinated in lime juice. Although he laughed at her squeamishness, he seemed, mercifully, to know better than to push the issue.

Although taking her first bite of solid food was an exercise in self-discipline, Adam Ryder's prediction was right. The lamb was fresh and delicate and she could feel her strength return with gratifying speed.

When, eventually, she sat cupping a mug of strong, soothing coffee in her delicate hands, she felt that she just might, after all, be able to cope with her new boss. He had been mostly silent throughout the meal, probably brooding over the bad luck that had saddled him with a woman given to fainting dead away in the middle of the street.

Running a long, buffed nail reflectively around the rim of her mug, she pondered her next move with him. She was determined to establish her credibility as a valuable employee after the morning's debacle.

'Josh gave me a general idea of what my assignment will be, Dr Ryder,' she began briskly, 'but given the circumstances, no details. It will be all whales, I take it. And quite technical.'

He didn't reply at once, but finished methodically tamping pungent tobacco into a bent pipe and bringing it to life with long, slow puffs. Then, 'Forget the "Doctor" bit, would you? My editor insists on putting it on my books, but other than that, I can't be bothered. It's Adam.... What do you know about whales?'

'Not a great deal,' she answered frankly. 'But I've sketched other animal life extensively—I'll show you samples from my case. As for the technical aspects, I've made rather a speciality of medical illustration lately. It shouldn't be a problem.'

'I trust not,' he said shortly. 'We won't have time for errors, considering the volume of work you'll have to produce. We've been studying one particular breed of whales here—the southern right whale. They were hunted almost to extinction at one time, and they still haven't made a very good comeback.'

He motioned the waiter for a refill of coffee. 'These waters off the coast of Patagonia are their mating and breeding grounds. They're only here for the short winter season—roughly July to November. I've been observing them for a couple of seasons. Got some good data on behaviour, population changes, anatomy ... which is where you come in, of course.'

'Are they the terribly big whales—Moby Dick and all that?' asked Jensa, warming to the actual subject of her work.

He gave a short, rather humourless laugh. 'Well, you may have left your winter coat behind, Jensa, but I see you packed your prejudices.'

Now what? she wondered. 'I don't understand ... Adam.'

He gave her a quick look. 'Forget it,' he said. 'It's just that most people still seem to think of whales as monsters—vicious creatures swimming about smashing boats and swallowing up latter-day Jonahs. If nothing else, I hope my book will help destroy these misconceptions which have contributed to their slaughter. But to answer your question—yes, they are large. Fifty or sixty feet. They can weigh around forty tons.'

'But how on earth do you study anything like that— surely it's very dangerous!'

'My point exactly when I first saw you,' he said, smiling ironically. 'It can be. But only if you don't know your business. But much of the time I just watch from the observatory, letting their activities tell me the story.

It's work that demands tremendous patience.'

Patience—from *this* man? she thought, but said, 'Can you really see that much of them from land?'

'More than you'd imagine. To start with, right whales have one advantage, in terms of study, over any other species. They have very distinct markings on their heads. We call them callosities—the old whalers used to call them bonnets. They're really a kind of whitish skin—very rough, and several inches thick. They're different on each one, so the whales become real individuals to us.'

'What do you look for as you watch them?'

'Breaching, spouts, lobtailing—everything. Then, with luck, over the months, or years even, we can begin to construct a picture of what their life is like in the deep ... they're magnificent creatures, you know!'

He talked almost emotionally about them, she thought, as she sipped her coffee and silently observed her companion. Apparently he tackled everything—people and work—fiercely. But there was a difference when he talked about the whales. The edges of the man were not quite so sharp or abrasive. Her mouth curved up in a hint of a smile in spite of herself.

'You're thinking something?' he asked.

'Yes—that you don't seem such an ogre when you're on the subject of whales. It sounds very much to me as if you like them a good deal better than you do mere human beings.'

'And you'd be right,' was his clipped reply.

'Well,' she ventured teasingly, 'I'll have to remember that, won't I?'

He didn't return her parry. 'As I said earlier, the research station is primitive at best. We're situated on private land—part of an enormous sheep ranch owned by a local businessman by the name of Felipe Mendez. He's allowing me to use a few old buildings that were once lived in by ranch hands.'

'A ranch—even a disused one—shouldn't be so bad,' Jensa offered breezily.

'Then you don't know this part of Argentina. It's been called the most desolate spot on the face of the earth. And in some ways it deserves its reputation. It's basically desert and rock sweeping right down to the ocean. And the dominating element is wind. Do you know much about its history?'

'Vague memories from school. There's a story, isn't there, about its name?' She willed herself to look directly into his still disdainful eyes.

'Yes—it means "big feet". Apparently when Magellan discovered it in the early 1500's, there were Indians living here. Very fierce and tall—they wore enormous boots stuffed with straw. They weren't fierce enough, however, and they were eventually exterminated. The Welsh came later, in the 1800's, to tend sheep. You'll still hear perfect Welsh spoken in Puerto Madryn, by the way. But the land was too forbidding, still is, to attract many settlers. There's coal and oil here, and that's bringing in more. But basically, where we're headed, it's virtually unpeopled.'

'It must be dreadfully boring for you at times, with nothing but whales to keep you company.'

'On the contrary. The solitary aspect suits me quite well. And while the land may seem desolate to most, I find it to be the most spectacular landscape in the world. The only thing I've never got used to is the winds—they're savage, and completely unpredictable ... where on earth do you get that colouring?'

Jensa blinked in surprise. The question was so off-topic, so personal, that she was momentarily flustered. 'Colouring?' she said faintly.

'Yes. Your hair, your skin. It's so fair it's hardly there.' From his mouth, it sounded almost like an accusation.

'Oh ... well, my father was English. He emigrated to Canada as a boy. And my mother was Scandinavian. Between the two of them, I suppose, I ended up this way. Washed out, you might say,' she said wryly.

'You'll raise some eyebrows around here. In fact, judging from the heads turned our way all through lunch, you already have.'

She supposed he considered it somehow unprofessional to look attractive. The eyes that held hers still showed mockery.

She shifted uncomfortably in her chair. She knew that many men found her particular type attractive. She'd been asked to model frequently throughout art school. Her long, abundant hair was like silver reflecting sunlight. Her fine, almost transparent skin showed just a blush of palest pink beneath the surface. She was just a touch taller than average, blessed with long legs and high, generous breasts. Her taste in clothes ran to classics in muted earth tones, with an occasional artistic flourish ... jeans and boots and sweaters for work, a simple black dress set off by a dramatic piece of antique jewellery for evenings.

'You look,' Adam Ryder added, 'artistic ... ethereal. Not up to scrambling over boulders at a research station.'

'I'm healthy enough, don't worry,' she retorted. 'And quite up to whatever you may throw my way, artistic or otherwise.' How tiresome, she thought. She recognised that look on his face and sighed inwardly. In addition to being a chauvinist and a bully, it looked as if he were a wolf as well. But she was experienced in fending off advances, although she supposed that when the advancer was your boss, the risks doubled.

As he turned his attention to paying the owner, Jensa studied him over the rim of her mug. His roughly chiselled features edged almost to homeliness—but stopped safely on the side of rugged good looks, she admitted grudgingly ... if you could ignore the atrocious manners. Which she couldn't, of course. There was nothing at all attractive about the type of man Adam Ryder had so far shown himself to be.

She noted critically how the months in such a harsh climate, much of the time probably spent on water, had marked him. His hands and face were coarsened and almost nut brown from exposure. The ragged hair at his temples was bleached almost to white.

The body and the personality were perfectly matched in aggressiveness, she thought. And she didn't like such men. Something the owner said caused him then to throw back his head and laugh, and as he did so, his eyes discovered hers on him. She flushed, but forced herself to return a casual smile.

'Time to go,' he announced abruptly. 'I don't like to leave the station for so long. Something could happen that might be important to the research.' The touch of his hand on her elbow as he steered her through the maze of small tables had an unsettling possessiveness about it. A man used to having his own way, she thought uneasily, and walked quickly on ahead of him.

The populated area around the port town quickly gave way to only scattered human settlements in the ranch country as they headed south. The deeper they went into Patagonia, the more closely it conformed to

Adam's dismal description. Jensa thought she had never before seen country so overwhelmingly stark. For mile after mile, the monotonous brown landscape was broken only by scattered outcrops of scraggly thornbushes.

And everywhere there were rocks showing the signs of the relentless winds of which he had spoken. It was not unlike being suddenly transported to the surface of the moon—or back into the darkness of pre-history. But she could see Adam's point—in its brutal way, the land did possess an almost mystical, timeless beauty.

'Does *anything* live here—Adam?' she asked, longing for the green of a shrub, or a flash of colour from a bird.

'On the contrary—this area abounds in unusual wildlife. We've got Darwin rheas, armadillos, guanacos. Keep looking. I'm surprised the artist in you doesn't have a keener eye for the drama of this land.'

The sarcasm in the voice told Jensa that she was being tested again—and found wanting, no doubt, she thought grimly.

'You can't deny,' she insisted, 'that it's not exactly a welcoming place.'

'So much the better. It keeps people out. Wherever people go, waste and destruction follow. People are just a bloody nuisance,' he said, expertly swerving to avoid a slide of rocks across the dirt road.

'I shouldn't think you'd be bothered by much human company no matter where you lived—you're not exactly welcoming yourself, you know,' she muttered, holding on to her seat for dear life.

'I could be ... if I take into account the purely decorative advantages of your presence.'

The suggestiveness in his voice stiffened Jensa's back

and sent a slight prickle running down her spine. She turned her head to one side and stared out at the broadening desert. He was still trying to unnerve her. And she had to admit that he was very close to succeeding.

'If you want, of course,' he went on, shifting into low gear for their descent down a rock-strewn hill, 'it's still not too late for me to turn around and have you on this evening's flight to Buenos Aires. All safe and sound back in civilisation!'

He was right, of course. There was still time. But she knew she wouldn't accept his offer—if indeed it had really been one.

'Not too late for me, perhaps,' she replied archly, 'but it certainly would be for you, wouldn't it! So spare me your games from now on, would you?'

'Ouch! You play a pretty hard game yourself for such a delicate-looking creature! Ah, well—perhaps it's all to the good. I can't afford to be distracted. Except on my own terms, naturally.'

She stared sharply into his enigmatic eyes. 'Just remember,' she said, now thoroughly picqued, 'I told you I could handle this situation as well as any man could, Adam. And that includes you!'

'I'm delighted,' he replied easily. 'I do hope you included something practical, and covering, to sleep in ... granny gowns, I believe they're called. We're rather cramped for space, you see. I had planned on Josh and me bunking together. Still insist on my not making any allowances for your sex?'

Jensa caught her breath and felt her eyes widen. 'You're an overgrown child, Adam!' she snapped. 'You think all this bluffing is going to panic me, providing you with some petty, small-minded amusement.'

'You can see for yourself whether or not I'm bluffing very soon. The station is just beyond that ledge of rock.' He slowed the Rover at the top of a shelf of yellowish, flaking rock.

She looked down and saw a cluster of dreary concrete block sheds huddled at the edge of a steep drop to a dark, wind-whipped sea.

'Well,' said Adam into the silence, 'would it be appropriate for me to say welcome?'

'Not exactly everyone's picture of a sleek, up-to-the-minute scientific facility, is it?' she said casually. 'Where are your technicians?'

'Technicians?' he said incredulously. 'Did I say anything about technicians?'

'Well ... no. Not directly. But Josh mentioned the ones you had out on Vancouver Island. And you yourself talked in terms of "our" research,' she said, striving to hold back her rising dismay.

He raised an amused eyebrow. 'You've assumed too much again, Jensa. I used local graduate students on the Vancouver project. I don't have a technician on this one.'

For the first time, the reality of her situation came crashing down on her. She had been so determined to keep this job, so offended by his offhand dismissal of her, that she had not really stopped to consider that the man might have valid reasons for not wanting her.

She whipped around in her seat and saw him drumming his finger on the dashboard, looking the other way. Alone. For a month. With this man? It was impossible ... utterly impossible!

CHAPTER TWO

JENSA drew a long, quivering breath. What now? she asked herself grimly. Insist that this smug, over-confident boor turn right around and drive her back to Puerto Madryn? Assuming that he would, she'd still have to face Josh and the depressing fact of losing the biggest assignment of her career.

The Rover bumped and lurched its way down the steep bank and came to a stop before a sagging veranda tacked on to the side of the characterless block building closest to the ocean. The engine stopped and Adam Ryder sat back, waiting to see what her next move would be.

Well, not what he had hoped for, she resolved. She'd show him she was made of tougher stuff than he had ever dreamed! She gave a crisp, impersonal smile, and began efficiently gathering her bags together. As she did, the door of the building burst open, revealing the short, rounded figure of an older woman, her dark face creased with a smile of greeting.

'Dr Ryder! Good to see you back—how was the trip into the city?'

Adam unfolded long legs-from behind the wheel and leapt to the ground with surprising lightness for a man so big.

'Interesting, Maria, interesting,' he replied in an off-hand manner. 'I've brought our illustrator back with me.'

The black eyes fell on Jensa for the first time, and

31

the smile vanished. Maria stared open-mouthed at her until Adam said, 'Mr Hager had an unfortunate involvement with an automobile, Maria, but has very kindly sent us a replacement. Jensa Welles, meet Maria Rodriguez. Maria keeps house for me, does what little cooking is required, or possible, in a place such as this.'

Jensa was as stunned by Maria's presence as the older woman was by hers, though she managed a warm smile and greeting. But even as she spoke to the woman, her mind was racing, thinking of the cheap trick Adam had played on her.

'Maria's husband José is with us, too,' he was saying easily. 'Does a million invaluable odd jobs, keeps the gears oiled, literally and otherwise. Here he is now,' he added, indicating a slight figure, nutmeg brown from a life lived in the sun, who was emerging from a small block hut on the other side of the yard. Judging from the heavy grease he was wiping from his hands, he had been at work on some piece of machinery.

The two men raised their hands in greeting. 'Things go all right while I was away, José?'

'Fine, Dr Ryder, no problems. No winds—and the whales, very quiet. I think they haven't got down to serious business yet!'

They laughed, and Adam said, 'Dear me, Miss Welles has taken me to task for forgetting my manners once today, and here I go forgetting them again!' He performed the introductions with José, who evidently shared his wife's shock. Jensa saw the two of them exchange raised eyebrows and shrugs of their shoulders. Like his employer, José apparently did not approve of her presence at their lonely little outpost.

Approve or not, thought Jensa, yanking a package

from the back of the Rover, they had her undying gratitude just for being here. Over firmly clenched teeth her eyes flashed a deadly look at Adam. He appeared to have totally forgotten her, and was deeply involved in a conversation with José about one of the boats.

It would be a long time before he scored another point at her expense, she thought. From now on, she'd be coolly efficient and do the job she'd come to do!

'You must be very tired after so long a trip, Miss Welles,' Maria said. 'Perhaps you'd like a cup of coffee and a rest now.' Her warm, concerned voice was like a blessing to Jensa and her shaky confidence.

Indeed she would, she thought—it had been a hard, dusty ride in the open vehicle, and she felt thoroughly chilled as well.

'I don't think that will be necessary, thanks, Maria,' came the hard voice behind her. 'Jensa had a rest after she got off the plane, and she's told me how eager she is to get started. Isn't that right?'

Jensa drew herself up to meet the implied challenge. 'Yes, of course,' she replied clearly.

'Up to a tour of the station?' The smile was icy, and left no doubt about what the only acceptable answer was.

'The sooner the better,' she replied brightly. Then, turning to Maria, 'Thank you for your offer—I'll be very glad to take you up on it a bit later on.'

Maria's eyes flicked apprehensively from one to the other. 'Of course,' she said quietly, then turned and disappeared into the gloom of the house.

Half skipping to keep up with Adam's long, impatient stride, Jensa followed him to the edge of the compound where a biting wind was beginning to blow

in, sharp with the tang of the ocean. 'That small building over there ... the one José was coming out of ... is
the maintenance shed. José has a bit of a shop there,
and keeps the Rover and outboard motors and such in
condition. Beyond it,' he continued, raising a long arm,
'is another old farm building. José and Maria have their
own private quarters in it.'

'Are they from Puerto Madryn?' she asked.

'No—they're on loan, you might say, from Felipe
Mendez. They do housekeeping and mechanical work
on the big ranch, but Felipe suggested that I might
find them of use out here. And I'm grateful. I couldn't
function without them.'

'This Señor Mendez,' asked Jensa, 'does he have
some special interest in whales—to be so generous with
his help, that is?'

'Felipe Mendez always has some special interest in
anything he decides to take a hand in,' he replied
cryptically. 'But in this case, I doubt very much that
it's the whales that have sparked his interest.'

'What, then?'

'Nothing that need concern you,' he said dismis-
sively.

On the far side of the main building stood an odd,
makeshift structure. A flight of alarmingly steep stairs
wound their way up to the top of a two-storey wooden
tower. It was topped by one tiny room, glass on three
sides, looking out to the sea.

'I'll be spending a fair amount of time up here,' said
Adam, taking the steps two at a time. 'This is my
observation post. You may have some use for it yourself, although your actual work space, out of necessity,
has been set up down in the main building.'

Jensa gave silent thanks for small blessings, as she

haltingly climbed the groaning steps. The thin, precariously leaning handrail offered scant reassurance. Adam loomed above her, watching her climb gingerly, a good deal of impatience in his stance.

'This is it,' he said, opening the door and indicating a cramped, plywood interior.

'Cosy,' she commented, eyeing the hard wooden seat set up before a large telescope, and the crude desk overflowing with papers, charts, and graphs. But if the surroundings were crude, the equipment most decidedly was not, Jensa observed, looking in astonishment at a polished array of telescopes, recording devices, and radar-like equipment. Accustomed as she was to the dazzling technology of the hospital, she was still impressed.

And if Adam Ryder himself, dressed in jeans that had seen better days and a sweater about to give at the elbows, looked casual and disorganised, his work was evidently anything but. The notes that she glanced at were written in a neat, decisive hand. The numbers were set down in meticulous columns. This was another side to her unpredictable employer, she thought.

'Let's see if we can find you something in the telescope now,' he said, crossing over to the powerful, floor-mounted machine. 'Perhaps one of my friends would be good enough to rise to the occasion, if you don't mind a bad joke.'

Any joke from you, she thought, would be a relief! Wisely, she kept her retort to herself. He sat perched on the edge of a tall stool, working the complex dials with strong, coarse hands that displayed surprising grace. He scanned the flat, grey ocean slowly. Moments later he reached out and grasped her wrist. 'I think we've got some luck. One of our younger, more exuberant ones is about to put in an appearance.' He drew her to the telescope and, one firm hand on the back of her head, pressed her face to where his had been.

'But I don't——'

'Patience, for heaven's sake!' he said sharply. 'If you're ever going to be of any use to me, you have to learn to wait for *them*!'

Jensa breathed deeply and peered harder into the lens. It was so unexpected when it happened that she cried out in a mixture of shock and wonder. A whale had suddenly breached. Even out there, in the limitless ocean with no reference points by which to judge its size, she knew it was enormous. Deep inside her, she was aware that she was in the presence of some form of life totally outside her experience.

'Oh! But it's impossible!' she breathed. 'Such things just can't exist!' In her excitement, she did a little bounce on the stool.

'Easy now,' he said calmly, 'you'll knock all this delicate equipment out of whack if you keep that up!'

'Sorry—it's just that I've never seen anything like it. It makes me feel kind of funny inside,' she explained. 'Will it come back?'

'Keep looking. Chances are that if he's done it once, you could be in for a bit of a show.'

Then, once again, she saw the surface of the water part and the great black back revolved smoothly upwards like a mammoth wheel. A giant plume of spray exploded from its blowhole. The deep, wheezing sound of its breathing rose up to the tower. Then, in an instant, it catapulted its tons of flesh into the air where it hovered before crashing seaward.

That such size could move so gracefully, seeming to glide without effort over the surface of the ocean! It raised goose bumps on her skin and instinctively she rubbed her arms. 'It's grand, isn't it,' she whispered.

'Yes,' he said quietly. 'There's nothing else in the world that can come close to it for such magnificence.'

Greatly daring, Jensa said, 'You don't suppose that little display is a sign that your whale friend is a great deal more pleased than the learned professor is about my appearance? I got the distinct impression that it would *love* its portrait done by me!'

'Perhaps,' he replied ironically, 'although it's my experience that whales do not share the human frailty of vanity. The boat there,' he continued, gesturing to the foot of the cliff, 'is the *Lightning*, a special pontoon outboard. I use it to go right out to the whales when I need to. It's specially designed for speed and manoeuvrability under difficult conditions. We do,' he added, smiling crookedly, 'have to move in a hurry sometimes out there.'

Jensa's eyes widened in amazement. 'You don't mean that you go out there——? You'd be only a speck next to them!'

'True. But as I said, these creatures, unlike many of their human cousins, are surprisingly gentle. They tolerate us, you might say, in the way you or I might tolerate the antics of a particularly pesky but harmless minnow while we're taking a dip.'

'Then you can get in quite close to them without danger?'

'Let's just say that if you know what you're doing, and wish them no harm, it's not particularly hazardous.'

'That's marvellous, then,' she enthused. 'I should be able to get some fantastic drawings of them. Could we go out tomorrow?'

He folded his arms across a broad chest. 'Now just

ease up there, my dear, and get one thing clear right
now. You work in the lab. Period. You'll not go anywhere near the boat!'

'But I thought you'd agreed to accept me fully as an
employee,' Jensa protested.

'I do,' he barked. 'As long as you stick strictly to
your duties. I won't have you risking trouble for the
project.'

'Fine—you're the boss, as you're so fond of reminding me. But I still feel you're hampering professionally.'

'In *art*, you're a professional. In the rest of it, you're
strictly an amateur! Do I make myself quite clear?'

'Crystal.' But to herself she resolved that before this
assignment was over, she'd have changed Adam
Ryder's mind on quite a few issues—and the boat not
the least of them.

'Let's get back to the main building,' he was saying.
'I suppose Maria will have supper ready for us soon.
After you,' he added, with heavy gallantry, indicating
the perilous flight of stairs.

The main building was little more than a cramped
cube roughly divided into areas of activity. There were
windows across one end offering an unobstructed view
of the ocean. There, one on either side of the room,
were two work tables. One, laden with material, was
obviously Adam's. The other, freshly tidied, Jensa
took to be hers.

To the other side of the entrance she could see a
tiny galley kitchen equipped with a propane stove. And
to the rear was a small alcove, curtained off by a piece
of bright cotton.

'Bed,' said Adam shortly. 'No indoor bathroom,
sorry to say. There's a facility of sorts out beyond the

work shed. Washing down we usually do right in the ocean.'

'That's fine,' she said breezily. 'You forget I'm from Montreal. Backwoods camping is something with which I'm quite familiar—and comfortable.' Despite the primitive nature of the accommodations, she noted that they were neat as a pin. That must be Maria's doing, she concluded. There was even the gay touch of a few native plants, potted in tin cans, growing in the windows. All in all, she decided, it was a good deal less cheerless than she had thought when she first arrived. She could, she thought, cope quite well, thanks to the heartening presence of Maria and José.

The evening's meal was waiting for them. In the pale apricot light of the oil lamps, Jensa and Adam sat on stools at the tiny wooden table.

'Maria's gone to great trouble for you tonight, I see,' said Adam. 'It's no small feat, I assure you, to bake a cake in the contraption we call our oven.'

'I'm flattered,' said Jensa, smiling warmly. 'And grateful. It smells absolutely delicious, Maria!' The dark-haired woman beamed as she set plates before them. 'But aren't they going to eat with us?' Jensa asked, seeing no plates were set for Maria or her husband.

'The Rodriguez' prefer to eat in their own house, usually,' he explained. 'I'm not one for long, leisurely meals. Most times I just have a sandwich at my desk.' He ladled out a spicy fish stew on to Jensa's plate. The fish had been caught that morning by José, and turned into a savoury feast by Maria's use of fiery spices. There was rice too, and, for dessert, Maria's cake.

Later, as they sat over strong coffee, talking more of the work they would begin the next day, Jensa became aware of an increasing heaviness in her limbs. She had been fighting sleep all evening, she realised. And now, with a warm meal in her, drowsiness was fast getting the better of her. Helped along by the warm glow from the iron heater, the long eyelashes swept her cheeks with increasing frequency.

'I take it you find all this slightly boring,' Adam interrupted her thoughts.

'I'm certainly not bored,' she found herself protesting. 'In fact, I'm amazed at how fascinating your material is!'

'You expected otherwise?' he asked, raising an eyebrow slightly.

'Well ... yes,' she admitted shyly. 'I had anticipated a rather cut-and-dried scientific study—not that you don't have all the technical data there. I can tell you've been very thorough. But you go so far beyond that!' For a moment she forgot her tiredness, and her expressive artist's hands came to life as she tried to convey to him how exciting she found the project.

You'll turn his head, she told herself finally. She looked up into his face, cocked to one side, the eyes slightly bemused. Her voice trailed off. No use in inflating *that* monumental ego, she thought. She tried to cover her agitation by busily stacking the coffee mugs on to a tray and studiously avoiding the eyes she knew were boring into her.

'You're tired,' he announced abruptly, pushing his stool back. 'Why don't you get your toothbrush and take yourself off to the privy? There's a flashlight right there by the door.'

When Jensa returned to the house, Adam was dragging a cot into the middle of the work area. She dropped her toilet kit on to the table and hurried to assist him with a pile of sheets that were slipping from under his arm.

'I'll be able to manage this from now on—you won't have to bother with it,' she said.

'This is for me,' he replied, positioning the cot between the two work tables. 'You'll sleep in the bed in the alcove—more privacy there.'

'Oh no,' Jensa said firmly. 'And then you'll feel justified in accusing me of stealing a good night's sleep from you as well as ruining your back! The cot is much better suited to a woman,' she insisted, imagining his great bulk crammed on to the flimsy frame.

'I thought you said you weren't going to take it upon yourself to argue with each and every decision I make! If I choose to complain to you, I'll complain. And I won't need to create an excuse to do it! Now, would you be kind enough—and smart enough—to get into your own bed. I should think you'd thank your lucky stars I'm willing to lug this thing out here every night, instead of making you take your chances in there with me, the way Josh would have.'

With that, he cast a frank eye over her body. To her horror, Jensa felt a blush flame her cheeks. That type of distasteful remark didn't merit a reply, but she couldn't stop herself. 'Oh, I'll go, all right. And I am grateful—grateful for every inch that separates us!' Chin lifted, she swung around and went into the alcove. She pulled the curtain closed with a jerk, trying futilely to shut out the amused guffaw from the other side.

So, she thought, your very first impression of the man was the right one. He was crude, ill-bred. There would be no winning with him.

'Don't forget—we start early,' she heard him call, the voice once again domineering and harsh.

'I'll be ready,' she replied shortly. And with that, the glow of the coal oil lamp flickered and died. Jensa was left to change into her nightie in darkness, and grope her way into bed. She lay there, utterly still, while images of gentle grey giants swam in and out of her dimming consciousness. She was pulled down, unprotesting, into a deep and restful sleep.

It was the aroma of strong South American coffee that finally pulled her out of her dreams. She awoke as groggy as if she had been drugged, confused for the moment about where she was. She supposed that it was still early, given the darkness of the windowless alcove. She groped for her watch and, struggling to bring her eyes into focus, read with alarm that it was past ten.

Good heavens! she thought, throwing back the covers, instantly awake. And I promised him I'd be up at the crack of dawn to start on the drawings. Tying her thin robe snugly about her waist to keep out the chill, she yanked back the curtain and blinked at the intense light which flooded the room.

'Good morning, Miss Welles!' came the greeting, in cheery, heavily accented English.

'Oh, Maria ... good morning,' she replied in a husky voice while her eyes frantically scanned the room for what she was sure would be Adam's scornful face.

The other woman, sensing the object of Jensa's wild-eyed search, said, 'Dr Ryder, he went early, as usual. He is always on the water by six. José helps him load the equipment while I make the breakfast. Here—come and sit while I get you something warm. It's very cold this morning!'

Jensa did not know, oddly, whether she felt relief or

disappointment. 'Thank you—I will,' she said, snuggling her feet down into her little travel slippers. Maria set steaming coffee, fresh orange slices, a fragrant spice bun on the little table.

'I feel so badly,' said Jensa, pouring tinned cream into her cup. 'I was supposed to get an early start, and here I am sleeping in like this!'

'You shouldn't worry—Dr Ryder himself instructed me to let you sleep as long as you wanted. You have a long trip to recover from, and a change in time, too, I think.'

'That's true . . . but I'm perfectly fine. I do wish he'd had you wake me!'

'He was very insistent. Said you would be all fuzzy unless you slept a long time.'

Typical, thought Jensa, sighing and breaking off bits of roll. Not done out of consideration at all—just concern that I shouldn't cause trouble. And unless I miss my guess, Adam will somehow manage to blame me.

Her eyes fell on a stack of papers and journals piled on her work table. 'Were those left for me, Maria?'

'Oh, yes! I was to tell you that he would like you to read them,' Maria replied, wiping the last of the morning's dishes.

'Well,' said Jensa, crumpling her napkin and rising, 'I'd best be at it—what time does he usually come in from the water, Maria?'

'José said he took lots of tape with him this morning. And the whales are very active. So maybe not till early afternoon.'

'Good,' said Jensa, pouring another mug of coffee and taking it back to the alcove. 'I'll be ready and waiting for him.'

She pulled the curtain across the arch and set the

paper bags containing yesterday's purchases on the bed.
It was still terribly cold in the block building, despite
the coal fire in the iron stove.

Shivering, she quickly slipped into jeans, a blue
checked shirt, and a heavy natural wool fisherman's
sweater. She brushed the pale blonde hair and braided
it neatly into a long plait which fell in a golden band
down her back. A flick of mascara and a dash of gloss
on her slightly pouting lips, and she felt trim and in
control.

Later, as she crossed the gravelled courtyard back to
the house, toilet kit in hand and towel across her shoulder, a flash of light caught her attention. Shielding her
eyes from the glare coming off the water, she spotted
the *Lightning* out in the bay. She could barely make
out Adam's small form and a tangle of equipment
spilling out of the rubber craft into the water.

With only a little more confidence than she had had
the previous day, she climbed the staircase and entered
the look-out tower. Careful now, she admonished herself. Mustn't upset any of this stuff! She adjusted the
powerful telescope and drew the *Lightning* into focus.

She could make out his features perfectly, and for a
moment felt her pulse quicken for reasons she could
not explain. She dismissed the flutter impatiently.

Adam was enclosed in a skin-tight rubber wet suit.
A black wool watch cap was pulled down low over his
brow so that except for his hands and face, he was entirely in black.

A set of headphones was clamped on him, and long
lines extended from the maze of electronic equipment
into the water. Listening to them? she wondered. She
watched fascinated as he picked up an oar and deli-
cately manoeuvred the craft around. The water was

very rough to Jensa's eye, and it was difficult to believe, despite his assurances, that the *Lightning* was capable of dealing with heavy seas.

Adam had said the whales were most active during stormy weather, almost as if they liked to play with gales that would bring terror into a human heart. Lost in concentration, he also seemed undaunted by the rising waves. But then, she reminded herself, Adam had seemed not quite human from the moment she met him.

As before, the breaching was totally without warning, and the shock was fresh. The sea erupted in a storm of spray and foam, and forty tons of glistening black flesh catapulted into the air mere yards from Adam. Jensa cried out, feeling sure that it meant sudden death for him.

But the ocean calmed beneath the leviathan, and it rested easily near the surface, looking straight at Adam.

She could see clearly the white encrustations on the broad head, the eyes, plus the most remarkable ear-to-ear grin that had the bizarre effect of making the whale look like a good-natured clown.

While she sat spellbound, Adam reached out and stroked the enormous face. Jensa could see that he was speaking to it. 'And probably a good deal more civilly than he does to mere humans,' she muttered.

With his other hand, Adam reached around and grabbed a microphone which he held near the surface of the water. 'Would you be kind enough to answer a few questions for this roving reporter?' she giggled to herself.

The scene she was watching both frightened and excited her for reasons she could not yet fathom. She was more sure than ever, now, that she must break

Adam down and get him to take her out with him. She *must* see these incredible creatures close up herself and then try to express on paper the emotions they aroused in her!

Fired with determination to set brush to paper, she carefully returned the telescope to the exact position in which she had found it and skipped down the steps, heedless this time of their alarming wobble.

By noon, she had lovingly unpacked her precious pens and inks, sable brushes and various qualities of paper. A neat row of tints and erasers and needle-sharp pencils marched across the top of her desk. Satisfied that everything was in meticulous order, she got down to business with the material Adam had left.

It was a prodigious task, and had she not already witnessed the awesome beauty of the whales herself, she might have found much of it dry and tedious. What this needs, she told herself, is for someone—me —to make this come alive!

From what she had read of Adam's work, he had that gift with words. Her drawings would complement it perfectly! Oh, there'd be lots of room for the exact, technical drawing—skeletons and tissue and such. But another dimension was needed, and she was so sure, now, that she could provide it.

She decided to mark a few places on his notes where some non-technical drawings could be inserted. She scanned the piles of complex charts and records on his desk. A large bulletin board on one wall held more technical material, plus a profusion of photographs. She smiled back at the same grinning face that she had seen through the telescope that morning and laughed aloud at the close-ups of faces that bristled with human-like moustaches and eyebrows. Her finger slid

from one picture to another, then stopped short at one
that seemed out of place indeed.

Dark eyes, looking up from under a fringe of long,
thick lashes, stared provocatively out at her. An off-
the-shoulder gown in fiery red exposed thin white
shoulders and the curve of full breasts. A cascade of
raven curls tumbled down her back. Jensa read the
large, flamboyant signature—*All my love, Rita*. The
'all' was underlined, she noted, wrinkling her nose in a
mixture of amusement and distaste at the obviousness
of the message.

The type Adam Ryder prefers, she thought ...
feminine and willing. One who knows her place and
doesn't try to intrude in serious matters like work. A
fiancée? she wondered. Hardly likely. He didn't seem
like the type who'd be capable of commitment to even
so luscious a creature. 'If she's any indication of what
he likes in women, it's no wonder he thought I'd be a
helpless nuisance!' She snorted in disgust and went on
with her work, dismissing the picture from her mind.

The porch door burst open, letting a blast of raw
air in, and Jensa looked up from her drawing board to
see Adam stride in, filling the cramped room with his
bulk and raw energy. He had changed out of his wet
suit and was back in the familiar jeans, stretched tightly
over muscular thighs, and a faded denim work shirt.

He yanked the watch cap off, releasing a shock of
sun-lightened hair over the brow, and tossed it into
a chair, saying, 'Morning—or afternoon—Sleeping
Beauty.'

She supposed he was laughing at her again, although
it was difficult to tell. His eyes were treacherously hidden behind dark aviator glasses. But when he removed
them, she saw the usual hostile expression. His glance

left out nothing. It slid from her hair, over the lines of her sweater, and lingered on the long expanse of her legs. Every bottle of ink and pencil seemed to be duly noted as well.

'I hope everything suits you,' she said, half annoyed and half nervous. She slid down off the stool and crossed to the kitchen. 'Maria left us some lunch—you must be starved by now!'

'You haven't eaten either?'

'No, I waited for you.'

They sat side by side on a battered, sagging couch, and Jensa set the plate of sandwiches on the crate which served as coffee table. As she poured his tea she found herself disturbingly aware of his body next to hers. He smelled slightly of the sea, clean and tangy, mixed with the richness of his tobacco. She tried to push her fascination aside, but maddeningly found her eyes drawn to a flash of gold in the thick hair at the base of his throat.

'Wondering what this is?' he asked, pulling a heavy gold chain and tiny white object from his open collar.

'Yes, I did notice it,' she admitted in a voice as casual as she could manage.

'It's scrimshaw—carved whalebone. Done years ago by a whaler during one of his long voyages.'

'I thought you didn't approve of whale hunts . . . and their products,' she commented, studying the minute carving.

'I don't. But it's too late to save the whale that this came from. And somehow I like having a piece of it near me . . . I feel a kinship with it. And I don't have it in for all those poor beggars who went to their deaths in icy waters two hundred years ago, you know, Jensa. Those men were miserable victims as much as their prey was!'

'And the modern whalers?' she asked, observing the intensity in him.

'It's not necessary, that's all,' he said with deceptive calm. 'You don't need to blast another living creature into agonising death just to make dog food, or give a bunch of women a smoother lipstick. It's just one more cruelty committed for the sake of vanity.'

'Women, I can see,' said Jensa coolly, 'come in for a lot of blame in your book, don't they, Adam?'

'Their fair share, no more, no less,' he replied evenly.

She redirected the conversation. 'I'd like to give you some ideas on the book that came to me this morning.'

'An instant expert?' he said, raising a sarcastic eyebrow.

'Not in a scientific way, of course,' she conceded. 'But as an artist, yes—I do have some very definite thoughts.'

'Let's not get in over our heads the first day. We'll get you warmed up on something fairly straightforward.' It was a thinly veiled dismissal of any original idea she might have, she realised, and her hand tightened involuntarily around her mug. If he intended to dictate every step of the artistic phase of the work, as well as lord it over her with that insufferable personality, they were in for an even tougher time than she had imagined.

'I want a technical drawing of the bone structure of the flipper. I have a good specimen from an autopsy I did a while ago. Not the queasy type, are you?' he asked, almost as if hoping she were. The implication of her weakness made her bristle.

'Not at all—my hospital work cured me of that,' she said confidently, but wishing all the same that she had forgone the rare roast beef sandwich.

It turned out to be not bad at all, just a small specimen preserved in a jar. It would be an easy first subject, she thought with relief.

'And when you're through with that, one showing the parallels between the whale foetus and the human foetus.'

'Where do you get these specimens Adam?' she asked, studying the rows of bottles in a cupboard. 'Surely you don't capture them?'

'Good lord, no. I use only what's washed up on the beaches, usually newborns that are defective in some way.'

Jensa listened to him attentively. Her nervousness was quickly waning as her enthusiasm for her subject increased. Adam's devotion to his work was infectious, she thought. He was a different person when he spoke about it. The hardness and cynicism drained away. Behind the rugged dress and less-than-gracious manner was a fully professional scientist with exacting standards. Obviously, he was going to demand the same from her.

She did not mind. She was used to giving her best. It was just that ... what? she wondered. That she had never before seen such changeableness in a man ... such a split between the man and the scientist. He was quite a paradox, this Adam Ryder.

Well, Adam, I can see why you're not married, she thought, as she watched his sharp eyes studying some notes intently. No woman in her right mind would subject herself to a man whose only real interest is his work, and who's nothing but a boor in his personal relationships.

'Do you understand——!'

'What?' she said.

'I said, do you understand, now, how I want these pages set up? You *were* listening to me, weren't you?'

'Of course I was,' she said, recovering. 'You want the brain studies there beside this section. The spinal studies follow that. And the foetal sketches will go in a separate section. Pen and ink.'

He looked at her hard for a second. 'Fine. How soon?'

Jensa cocked her head and bit the end of her pencil, considering. 'Two days should do it, with any luck. How does that work out for you?'

'No problem. I'll talk to you about the next lot when you're done with these. Any questions?'

Something prompted her to flirt with danger, and later, she couldn't imagine what had made her do it. It was stupid. 'One ... why is it that you like animals so much better than you do people?'

'I've got lots of reasons.' He spoke with deliberate, studied patience. 'You won't find these creatures spoiling their environment. They're loyal, affectionate, sensitive. We humans could learn a good deal from them. But we set ourselves up as worthy of deciding which creatures will live and which will die!'

Jensa flinched, regretting the rashness of her question. It pleased him to think that he had frightened her, she realised a little wildly. You're a dangerous man to be around, Adam, she thought. And the sooner I finish and get out of here, the better!

'You no doubt think I'm some kind of fanatic,' he observed.

She steeled herself to respond to him. 'Yes ... I do think your views are extreme. I agree with you that man has done some pretty terrible things, but I don't condemn all men because of it. But you're entitled to your view, just as I am to mine. So it's really no concern to me one way or another, you see!'

'I see many things, my dear, including the fact that you are a very beautiful woman. It's a pity that you and I have been brought together professionally. This could be a fairly interesting interlude, otherwise.'

With that cynical announcement, he leaned his body over her and pressed her back on the sofa, covering her mouth with his, brutally forcing it open. When at last he released her, he said, 'I did that to shut you up—you push me too hard, you know.'

He withdrew his body from hers, leaving her shaken and unable to reply. But when she looked up into those cold, mocking eyes, her response came in full. She brought her hand across his face with a sharpness that drew colour to his cheek and pain to her hand.

His hand flashed out and caught her wrist, pinioning it to the seat. 'An appropriate reaction, Miss Welles, and well done. But I know women who look like you love such attention ... even though they all feel obliged to go through with these little charades of mock outrage.'

'I can assure you, Dr Ryder, that my outrage is not a sham! You will *not* treat me in such a manner as long as I'm here—do you understand? I will not be an "interlude" for you or any other man. If you ever try that again, I'll leave you and your precious project high and dry—even if it means hiking back across that godforsaken desert alone! Do I make myself clear?'

'Oh, very!' he said, laughing unpleasantly. 'That's a very outraged little production. I could almost believe it—if I hadn't already felt the response in your lips.'

Jensa sat sputtering in futile rage while he stood, as if nothing untoward had passed between them, and immersed himself in a pile of graphs on his desk. Not two minutes later, a bomb could have gone off in the room and he wouldn't have noticed it, so great was his absorption in his work.

It was with a tremendous exercise of will that Jensa smoothed her hair, straightened her sweater, and walked to her table with slow, controlled steps. Like a robot, acting yet not thinking, she carefully laid out paper, pens, an enamel specimen tray.

She bent her neck over the table and frowned in concentration at the delicate tracery of the flipper bones. Maddeningly, her attention was drawn repeatedly to the man across from her who laboured in total concentration, unaware of her existence.

She heard papers rustle, pens drawn firmly across pages, the scritch of a match being lit by a thumbnail. He was so utterly self-possessed, so silent, and yet his presence screamed at her.

You're despicable! she fumed silently. To kiss a woman in a way that almost destroyed reason obviously meant nothing to him. Are you still trying to frighten me? she wondered. Trying to get me to pack up and run away like some scared child so you can be free to find a man for the project? Well, you can think again. I won't give you that satisfaction in a million years.

She wondered suddenly about the picture pinned just above his head, the one of the dark and beautiful woman who smiled down on him so seductively. She imagined Adam kissing her and shook her head as if to rid herself of the image. She felt a flick of something in her breast, something perilously close to jealousy.

This is unbelievable, she lectured herself harshly. Just because you're out here in this wasteland is no reason to forget who you are—or what you believe in!

But that night she lay not breathing as she heard his footsteps on the other side of the flimsy curtain that separated their beds. Had he stopped there? What if he decided to pull that curtain aside and press his demands on her again? She felt her pulse quicken in that vulnerable spot at the base of her neck that his lips had brushed after he kissed her. But the footsteps receded and he did not come. Jensa stared up at the darkness for well into the night.

CHAPTER THREE

ONE hand darted out, grabbed the watch, and retreated into the blissful warmth of the blankets. Six-thirty, she read. Good. Adam would be out on the water by now, and she could get a good start on the next set of drawings.

She rose, stretched, and smiled sleepily. Trailing her robe behind her, toilet kit in hand, she pushed through the curtains and stopped short. It was Adam's back bent over his desk that greeted her instead of Maria's cheerful round face. He turned slowly and raked her from top to toe with his eyes.

'Morning,' he said easily.

Jensa looked down quickly at the thin material of her gown which barely covered the soft lines of her body, flushed, and quickly belted her robe about her. It was disconcerting to think that he had been sitting there, working calmly, while she slept on the other side of the flimsy barricade. It seemed to place him, as usual, in the dominant, controlling position he relished. He had undone, in one second, all the poise with which she had been determined to face him that day.

She mustered a cheerful, offhand smile. 'Morning! I thought you'd be long since gone.'

'Winds are coming. Only an idiot would go out there today. And I'm not an idiot.'

Jensa crossed to the windows and peered out into the murky rose of the early morning. 'Things seem pretty normal ... a little grey, perhaps.'

She heard him give a snorting little laugh. 'We've got a good one blowing in ... you'd better be off and do whatever it is you do to get yourself ready for the day, before things get rough.'

Jensa felt warmth rise in her face at the hint of intimacy in the comment, and headed quickly for the door.

She returned to find Adam had placed coffee and rolls and fruit on the crate. 'Sit,' he commanded. 'We'll be working together today. Let me see what you've done so far.'

Jensa placed a pile of drawings between them on the sofa, and watched as he poured coffee into generous pottery mugs. As he bent over the crate, she noted the sleeves of his sweater roughly pushed up to reveal muscle-ridged forearms, the leather knife sheath snapped to his belt hook, a horn-handled knife protruding aggressively. His thighs were spread carelessly to take up half the sofa.

Jensa felt a stab of physical attraction hit squarely in her abdomen and quickly she averted her face. In no way could she allow herself to feel any sort of attraction—least of all an intimate one—for a man of this sort.

He turned to her, offering a mug, and she accepted it, lowering her lashes.

'Now,' he said, 'let's see what you've got here!' He went through them slowly, painstakingly, while Jensa toyed nervously with her pastry, all appetite suddenly vanishing. His face betrayed not a hint of what he might be thinking about her work.

Shame on you! she scolded herself silently. You're no green beginner begging for approval—you're a seasoned pro. Your work is first-rate. But the butterflies fluttered, unconvinced.

Impulsively she stood and crossed to the iron stove with its circle of warmth. She turned her hands this way and that over it, painfully aware of each dragging second. She had figured Adam would be as quick to make judgments in this as he was about everything else. But she should have known better. When it came to anything that affected this project, he was meticulous.

He raised his coffee to his lips, then began the slow ritual of filling his pipe, tamping it down, lighting it with slow, deep puffs.

'What's all this stuff at the back?' he asked finally.

Despite her anxious waiting, Jensa was caught off guard. 'What stuff . . .?' she stammered.

'The pages in the separate folder at the back,' he said, as if he were talking to a particularly difficult child.

'Oh!' she said, relieved and agitated at the same time. She returned quickly to the sofa. 'Pictures of tailing or flopping or whatever you call it!'

'Lobtailing,' he said, quietly exasperated.

'Right,' she agreed, passing over the irritation in his voice. 'Lobtailing.'

'But that wasn't your assignment.'

'I know,' she said, not feeling the least repentant. 'But the anatomical studies are all there, too. The others I did earlier in the day.'

'Earlier? When?' he demanded.

Jensa sighed and steeled herself for yet another go-round with him. 'Yesterday,' she began with delibera-tion, 'after I went up to the tower to see if I could spot you. And I did. Then the whales appeared—I thought it was all so thrilling I had to come back here to get my impression down right away. They're quick sketches, nothing detailed ... I only meant to capture their power and grace. You know how they combine it so uniquely!'

'Yes, I know,' he agreed sardonically.

She continued tentatively, 'So, as I said, they're only rough. But I was hoping you'd want them to supple-ment the technical stuff. As soon as I read your text I knew what was needed. I mean, your story isn't just dry data—it's really a very passionate plea for the right of these creatures to life. You said so yourself!'

'Yes, I did,' he replied, watching her with an ex-pression she could not define. 'Go on.'

'Well ... that's it, really.' She sat before him expect-antly.

He removed the pipe from his mouth, paused, and said slowly, 'They're very good. I was shocked to see them, that was all. I only expected the anatomical work.'

'Gosh, I'd forgotten all about that—are they all right?'

'They're very fine. Clear, precise, yet attractive. If you do all the rest in this fashion, I'll have no com-plaints.'

Jensa allowed herself to exhale very slowly. Just for

the moment, the ice seemed to be broken between them. It was pushing her luck, she supposed, but she had to ask. 'And the others ... do you think you'll use them?'

It was obviously difficult for Adam Ryder to praise anyone. Or share responsibility with them, she thought, watching the tightness about his jaw. 'I think,' he said finally, 'that we might find a place for them.'

It wasn't much. Hardly the roaring enthusiasm she herself felt for the pictures. But considering the nature of the man, he had said a lot. She bent her head quickly to sip at her coffee before her dimpling cheeks could betray her delight.

There was one thing more she wanted to say. 'I think,' she tossed out casually, 'that if I'm to get some really good material—not just rough things like these— that I'll have to be in a better position to study them.'

'What did you have in mind?' he asked, folding one long leg over the other and leaning back to take in all of her.

'The boat. Now I know what you said, but how else can I get close?' He raised a hand, but she pressed on. 'It's the only *way*, Adam! Surely you can see now just how valuable it could be to the project?'

The relative amiableness of the morning vanished in an instant. 'I thought I had made myself clear, Jensa,' he said very, very quietly. 'I don't like repeating myself, but I'll say it once more. You're here only because of circumstances—and damned unpleasant ones. You'll do what I pay you to do. Stay away from my equipment. And if you go anywhere near that boat, I'll forget you're a woman and take a more direct method of dealing with you.' One strong hand patted the back of the sofa symbolically.

I wish he'd shout at me, she thought furiously. I'd much prefer it to that superior, icy calm! Sensing that this was one particular mountain she was not going to move ... not this morning, at least ... she squelched the sharp reply that was on the tip of her tongue and settled instead for replacing her mug on the crate with a good deal more force than was necessary.

'I'm sure slamming things around is good for your psyche, Jensa,' he remarked with maddening calm, 'but I would prefer that you pour those energies into this morning's work.'

Idiot! Did he really think he had to continue with this lord and master routine? She shot him a look of pure defiance. Art—that was her territory! And she fully intended to guard her authority in that area just as fiercely as Adam protected his in every other area.

She crossed the room with long, angry strides, plunked herself down on the stool and sat perfectly still.

'Now what?' he asked, surveying her with his head cocked to one side.

'I'm waiting,' she replied. 'To be told what to do. Of course, you should understand that you'll be getting third-rate work. You always do when you try to dictate all the spontaneity out of an artist. But then this little cinder block compound is your own private kingdom, isn't it? Big, bad Adam is king, and always gets his way, whether his way has any sense or merit whatso-ever!'

'I am delighted that at last you understand,' he said, easily. 'I was afraid you hadn't got the message yet.' He went to the cupboard and pulled out several speci-men jars.

'Foetuses,' he said. 'And some glands. Just carry on

with these the way you did the others. As I said, they were quite satisfactory.'

'Why, thank you,' breathed Jensa, one hand pressed to her breast in mock surprise and humility.

He studied her for a few moments and then said, 'You know, if you'd unbend just a little, perhaps we could take a little more pleasure in each other's company.'

She looked at him quickly. 'If you're referring to the other night, and that most unwelcome gesture, you can forget it. You think along very narrow lines when it comes to women. And I for one am simply not interested in a relationship that's just a passing physical fancy.'

'You're the serious type, then ... commitment, constancy, and all that,' he said. His tone was mocking.

'Why should that surprise you? There are still some of us antediluvian creatures around, you know.'

'I suppose I find it hard—no, impossible—to believe that a girl who looks like you do hasn't had more than her share of physical attention from men. And enjoyed it, unless you're made of pretty frigid stuff. But that I discount, given the response I felt when I kissed you.'

'How shallow!' she snorted. 'I can't help my appearance. In fact, there have been times when I've considered it a liability. It can attract very undesirable attention ... and people,' she added, looking unblinkingly at him. 'I think the problem lies decidedly with you, when you treat whales with a good deal more sensitivity than you do women.'

'I treat women in the manner they both want and deserve. And so far, I have not lacked female companionship in my life. I admire a woman who knows how to give pleasure. And can be honest about it.'

'Honest!' she laughed. 'Oh, do spare me that tired line!'

'I happen to believe it,' he returned. 'I much prefer a woman who doesn't bore me to death spouting nonsense about eternal love and devotion.'

'Pathetic,' said Jensa, shaking her head. 'Very pathetic. I can imagine where you pick up such creatures. Now, if you don't mind, I'm beginning to find this conversation both tedious and distasteful. I'd like to get to work on these specimens!'

They worked for the rest of the morning in silence. Jensa was acutely aware of the undercurrent of friction between them, but at least had the warm pleasure of seeing delicate pictures gradually emerge from the blank pages before her.

Gradually, almost imperceptibly, the room darkened. At one point Adam rose to light a coal-oil lamp to help Jensa with the detailed work she was doing. Maria appeared briefly, singing softly to herself in a high, sweet voice. She left their usual lunch of sandwiches and fruit. Jensa caught brief glimpses of José scurrying about in the yard putting equipment safely away in sheds, taking extra rope down the cliff to tie the *Lightning* more securely.

Brief, intense squalls appeared and whipped the surface of the ocean into peaks of white. The sound of the wind rose into a high whine around them, and Jensa snuggled herself farther down into the depths of her sweater.

She had always rather enjoyed a storm. It was a deliciously cosy feeling being safe inside while it raged outside. Gradually, she became aware of another sound mixed with the wail of the wind—something lower, richer, almost ghostly. She laid her pencil down and strained to hear it.

She turned to him, a question on her lips, and saw that his eyes were already on her, as if anticipating the question. 'Yes,' he said, 'it's the whales. It's always more intense during one of these blows.'

'But why—what are they doing?'

'After all this time, we still don't really know exactly. All we can really say for sure is that they love the wind ... revel in it. In a really good one, they like to go sailing.'

'I see,' she laughed, 'hoist their jibs and set their mainsails and all that!'

'Don't be so quick to laugh, my dear. You're not far wrong. They do, in fact, raise their tails and use the force of the wind to take them for rides.'

Jensa turned her head back to the Atlantic and saw that indeed the sea was churning with a restlessness that the winds alone couldn't explain. She was off her stool in a flash. 'Can we go out? I *can't* miss something like this!'

He hesitated a second, then nodded. He followed after her as she hurried down the front steps and across the yard in the direction of the ocean. He kept easily abreast of her with his long, firm stride, and wore a faint, wearied smile on his face, as if he were indulging some capricious child.

Breath was knocked out of Jensa as she reached the cliff. Here there were no buildings to break its fury, and the wind swept in off the sea untamed. She surveyed the barren landscape littered with time-worn pebbles and felt she understood for the first time what sweeping hand had moulded this old land.

Bent almost double against the wind, the two of them struggled the last few feet to the edge of the drop, where they had the best view of the foaming seascape before them. Adam stood, one long leg angled out before the other to brace them against the wind. Instinctively, he had placed himself between Jensa and the full brunt of the wind. She experienced a stirring gratefulness for his superior stamina, that brought a not unpleasant warmth to her.

Cupping her hands to protect her eyes against the gritty gusts, she stared out into the Atlantic to where the maelstrom was in full swing.

'That one—the biggest fluke,' shouted Adam over the wind, 'that's Beau!'

'Because he's beautiful?'

'Nothing so romantic—I named him after Rear Admiral Sir Francis Beaufort—inventor of the Beaufort Wind Scale! Beau's always the first to set sail, last to pull it down.'

'A regular ski bum of the nautical variety,' she shouted. She watched with delight as Beau's massive tail rose high out of the water and turned until it was at right angles to the wind. He caught it, and the dark mountain of flesh was carried landward at a rapid speed.

The sail over, the young whale performed the equivalent of a teenage boy's whoop of joy. He leapt and slapped the water with a thunderous explosion of surf. Then, the rambunctious lobtailing over, he circled for another run at the shore.

'I wish I could sketch it right here,' she said, 'but the paper would be whipped right out of my hands.'

'Do you really think you could capture the movement and the power of all this?'

'I think I'd like to give it a good try!' she shouted back enthusiastically.

'I talk about this in the book. An illustration would

be fine—I just never thought I could get one to do the scene justice.'

'Did you ever consider photographs?' she asked.

'Yes—but it's practically impossible to get a clear shot with all this buffeting and spray. Give it a go, will you?'

Jensa nodded, unable to speak as a gust of wind hit her squarely in the face. The punishing wind pummelled them in earnest now.

'Come on!' shouted Adam. 'It's getting dangerous. I shouldn't have let us stay out here this long—we're far too exposed!'

'Just a few minutes more, Adam,' she cried. 'I want to get it fixed firmly in my mind!' She placed a protesting hand against his sweater as he reached out for her.

'Come on,' he repeated. 'That's an order!' And just as he spoke, a monstrous gust swept under them and threatened to lift Jensa off her feet. She would have been tossed like a stick over the edge had it not been for the lightning-quick speed with which Adam thrust one strong arm around her waist and heaved them both away from the lip of the drop into the water.

Adrenalin pumped through her, constricting her throat and making her heart beat painfully as she clung to the arm which hurt her terribly, so tightly did it hold her to his side.

Bent to the waist, heads downward, they struggled towards the compound. Adam half dragged her as she slipped and slid before the gale. 'This is precisely why I didn't want you here!' he bellowed. 'I knew you'd have a lot of hare-brained impulses that would make you go dashing off into lord knows what danger. And I'd have to risk my skin to get you out of it!'

Jensa's hair flew wildly about her face, obscuring

his from her, but she could hear the snapping anger in his voice. He was on the verge of another of his towering rages, but she didn't care. She was getting a little weary of Adam Ryder and his black furies! The adrenalin provided her with all the false courage she needed.

'You did agree to take me out in this, don't forget, Adam,' she taunted him.

'That's one mistake I don't intend to repeat!' Both hands held her slender shoulders in a vicelike grip as he hauled her upright before him. He slid his hands up her neck and smoothed the veil of silver back from her face and held it immobilised. 'I want you to go into the house while I find José to check on the equipment. You are to *stay* there. Is that understood?'

She felt her soft form brush against his hard muscles, tightened even further by his urgency. 'For heaven's sake, Adam,' she shouted, 'you've made your point—you don't have to maul me!'

'With you, Jensa, ordinary measures don't always have their desired effect. Tell me again—do you understand that you are not to come out into this again without my permission!'

Part of her wanted to rebel and break away from him. But another, persistent part craved contact with the unyielding body that had saved her, and would gladly have stayed in that rough embrace. 'All right!' she shouted, as angry at herself as she was at him. 'Just let go of me, you bully!'

He held her for another second, his eyes boring into her. Then he released her and strode off towards the tool shed, his jacket flapping wildly.

The wind continued in its fury until well into the afternoon. Jensa remained in the snug confines of the main building, warming herself with mugs of strong tea. She sketched in a frenzy of enthusiasm on the drawings of Beau while she still had the screaming of the gale to inspire her.

She seldom saw Adam—he came in only briefly to warm himself with tea. He and José were kept busy with an endless battle to secure equipment that threatened to tear loose and follow the wind westward.

At one point, the roof boards groaned ominously and seemed doomed to lift off entirely. Jensa watched anxiously as the two men, resorting to crawling on their hands and knees, struggled to secure ropes to the eaves.

And then as if tiring of its game with whales and humans, the storm vanished. Stillness settled in over the little compound. There was complete silence, except for the tapping of Adam's hammer from the top of the observation tower where he was repairing some loose boards.

Jensa paused in her work to rub at her neck, stiff from the hours over the board. Stretching luxuriously, like a beautiful blonde cat, she curled one leg under her and scanned the landscape for signs of destruction. But in a place of no trees and almost no buildings, there was very little sign that a storm had passed their way.

But there was something over there on the horizon. She couldn't make out what it was, but she was sure that it hadn't been there before. It appeared to be moving, coming towards them from inland. She slid down off the stool and went to the window.

For a long time it remained a vague speck on the horizon, trailing a thin line of dust behind it. But as it turned and began the descent to the shore, she could see clearly that it was a car and she felt a strange sense of excitement that they were to have a visitor here where hundreds of miles stretched between people.

As it plunged down the final hill to the compound Jensa blinked in astonishment. This was no Land Rover, or sane, battered farm vehicle. It was a sleek red Mercedes sports car. About as appropriate here, thought Jensa, as a ball gown in a chicken coop! She craned her neck to see who the intrepid—if foolish—driver was. Perhaps it was this important patron, Felipe Mendez!

There was an enthusiastic shout of greeting followed by the sound of Adam descending from the tower, two steps at a time. He rounded the corner of the building waving in obvious pleasure. Jensa watched as he opened the car door, reached down, and carefully handed out the driver, on whom he promptly planted a vigorous, lingering kiss.

'Well, well,' she said aloud, 'it's true. Not *all* women come in for Dr Ryder's scorn!'

The two appeared, moments later, arm in arm, the girl chattering animatedly in heavily accented, husky English.

'One of our ranch hands heard on his radio transmitter from one of the sheep stations that it had been very bad down here. So naturally I just had to come and see that you are all right! And anyway,' she chided him gently, 'I don't get to see very much of you now—even though I know for a fact that you passed near us when you went up to Puerto Madryn!'

'A thousand pardons, darling,' he said, grinning. 'But you know we're making the big push to complete the research. It's not that I haven't wanted to see you....' He gave her upturned chin a little tweak as if to placate her, and she laughed approvingly.

Jensa rolled her eyes heavenward at the display of

flirtatiousness. What a fine sight it was to see the severe Dr Ryder fawning like a love-struck adolescent! She gave a sarcastic little cough to remind him of her presence.

The girl turned the dark eyes on Jensa for the first time and looked at her with blank astonishment. Recovering, she turned questioningly to Adam, the dazzling smile once again lavished on him. 'I came also to meet this Josh of whom you spoke so admiringly—perhaps he has brought an assistant?'

'Not exactly,' said Adam guardedly, draping an arm around her shoulders. He explained briefly the circumstances of Josh's accident and Jensa's subsequent hiring. 'Jensa, I'd like you to meet Rita Mendez.'

Yes, thought Jensa. It was the girl in the picture—there was no mistaking her. There was no red dress this time, of course, and no bared shoulders. But the flowing raven hair was there, and the bright slash of the red-painted mouth. (Which had left its mark, Jensa noted, on Adam's.) She was dressed casually but expensively, in a short lambskin jacket and good wool pants topped by a bright silk blouse.

'Mendez,' said Jensa pleasantly. 'I've heard the name before. Are you related to the gentleman who owns this land?'

'Señor Mendez is my father,' came the dismissive reply. She shrugged off her jacket into Adam's waiting hands. 'It is most unfortunate about Josh,' she said, sitting on the sofa and patting the spot beside her as an invitation to Adam. 'But how lucky you are that he was able to send someone in his place! Tell me, Adam, does Miss Welles make a suitable employee?' She smiled, her small, even teeth gleaming very white against the dusky skin.

'Oh, most suitable,' agreed Adam, his voice heavy with irony. 'Follows instructions to the letter!'

'Perhaps, then,' cooed Rita, 'you wouldn't mind making some coffee, Miss Welles? It was a very long, dusty drive, and Adam and I have so much to catch up on!'

'Of course not,' said Jensa. 'I'd be delighted.' She smiled at Rita and looked at Adam with eyes that threatened murder. Play me off against her, will you, Adam? Not on your life! She crossed to the galley kitchen and pumped the little stove to light it, pointedly ignoring the laughter and chatter that came from behind her.

'You'll join us, won't you?' asked Adam later as she set the tray of coffee before them.

'Thanks, but I believe I'll keep my nose to the grindstone like a good little employee,' she replied breezily. She poured herself a mug and took it to her desk where she tried, without success, to shut out their conversation.

It was obvious that theirs was a relaxed and close relationship. Rita spoke to Adam with the possessive tone of a woman who has been on intimate terms with a man. The meaning of much of what she said was so blatant that Jensa practically shuddered with distaste. But to her surprise, she found herself reacting to the almost sure knowledge of their closeness with stomach-tightening tension.

For a man whom she believed to be obsessed with whales, she noted sourly, Adam was quick to abandon the topic when Rita tired of it. And for a man who was given to allowing doors to slam in her face, he was quick to jump to Rita's assistance at her feminine protestations of helplessness.

Conversation soon turned to mutual friends in Buenos Aires and the start of the new social season, of which Rita, it appeared, was a shining light—but surely this could not be another side of her unpredictable employer! Dressed in his crumpled work clothes, it was impossible to imagine him even approaching a civilised appearance.

'Does it bother you that I watch you work, Jensa?' Rita's voice broke into her thoughts. Adam had gone to reset a piece of automatic recording equipment, and Jensa turned to see Rita looking over her shoulder.

'No, not at all,' she replied evenly. 'If you're interested, I'd be happy to show you what we're doing.'

'I'm so glad,' came the smooth reply. 'I thought you might feel uncomfortable about showing your work to strangers. Adam tells me that you are only a student of the man he had hired.' The smile was sweet, but Jensa felt the stab.

'*Was*,' she corrected lightly, 'but that was some time ago. Anyway, as a professional artist, I'm quite accustomed to people inspecting my work.'

The girl picked up a stack of drawings with a carelessness that made Jensa wince. She flipped through them with hands that displayed long, scarlet-painted nails.

'They're very fine, my dear,' she gushed. 'There was no need at all for Adam to worry so!' With that back-handed compliment, she tossed the pages, already forgotten, back on the desk.

'You will soon be gone from here?' she asked.

'In a few weeks. But with luck,' Jensa replied, 'a good deal sooner.'

'It must seem like an eternity to you in a place like this. Tell me, where has Adam stuck you in these tiny quarters?'

Jensa sighed, put down her pen, and decided to meet the implication head on. 'Adam puts a cot out here in the work area every night. I sleep in the bed in the alcove. With the curtain drawn. It's really quite private,' she added firmly.

'I see,' said Rita slowly.

I'll bet you do, thought Jensa, but she bit back a reply. Trading insults with this tiresome girl was hardly a rewarding activity.

'Still,' Rita went on, pouting slightly, 'I feel Adam has put you in a difficult spot. I mean, it does not somehow look ... correct, that the two of you share the same house.'

'To whom?' laughed Jensa coolly. 'This isn't exactly a populous area. And even if it were, I'd have nothing to apologise for. Maria and José are here and everything is quite proper.'

Rita considered for a moment, then brightened. 'That is the solution, of course! You could sleep with Maria, and José could stay here with Adam. Frankly, Jensa, I am surprised that you did not think of it yourself.'

Jensa had a brief, amusing vision of her and Maria sharing the sagging double bed she had seen in the other building.

'Rita,' she said, summoning all the amiability at her disposal, 'Adam and I work very long hours—it wouldn't be right to impose them on the Rodriguez's. But quite apart from any hardship we might cause them, the fact is that my sleeping accommodation is of absolutely no concern to me.'

The mask of pleasant concern was dropping from Rita's face. 'I only hope my father can see your point,' she said. 'He is a very old-fashioned man in many ways. I don't know how he will feel about having an inexperienced woman in such dangerous surroundings. This was not part of the agreement when he consented to Adam's setting up the research facility on our property.'

Jensa hadn't expected this. A woman's jealousy was one thing. But surely her presence here couldn't cause any serious problems for Adam! 'I don't see how he could reasonably object,' she said. 'After all, I'll be gone from here in such a short time.'

'Let us hope so. My father is opinionated—he has never liked women who venture into men's work.'

They stood before each other, both silent, observant. Their exchange of looks lasted only a moment before the polite voices and guarded expressions returned. But it had been enough. Not a word had been said, but Jensa now understood the situation exactly.

Really! she thought in exasperation. That she should have been put in such a position with a woman like that! It was utterly absurd. And the arrogance of her! She wished she could tell Rita Mendez right to her smug, rich-girl face that she had no designs on Adam Ryder. They were welcome to each other!

The sweet smiles of goodbye couldn't have fooled anyone—except, she supposed, Adam. Breaking her promise to herself, Jensa watched as he and Rita strolled arm in arm out to the little red car, heads inclined towards each other. Adam bent over the car to place a lingering kiss on Rita's receptive lips, and the point of Jensa's pencil snapped and dug into the page.

Darn! A perfectly good drawing ruined. And it's *your* fault, she admonished herself, for giving in to idle curiosity! The car started up with a throaty roar and shot away at a ridiculous speed. Rita drove exactly as Jensa had predicted—with a scattering of gravel and too much noise. Rita Mendez, she decided, never did anything in less than an attention-getting manner.

Adam watched until the rear of the Mercedes disappeared over the first hill, then turned and hurried into the house. Jensa busied herself with some sketches, assuming as casual an air as possible.

'Well,' he said easily, 'I'm glad you and Rita hit it off.'

Jensa smiled sweetly. 'We have so much in common.'

He gave her a quick look. 'Do I detect a hint of cattiness in that reply, Miss Welles?'

Jensa sighed. 'You know darn well you did, so let's not waste our time by playing games. I'm sure Miss Mendez conveyed to you exactly the same message that she did to me—that she's not at all pleased to see me here.'

'I'm sure her reaction was no different from mine. When you come prepared for six feet, two hundred pounds, and a sandy beard, and find instead——' He gestured in her direction.

'I'm sure the two of you had a good time commiserating with each other,' she said acidly.

'Mustn't get snippy, now, Jensa,' he chided. 'It's not at all becoming. Tell me truthfully—what did you think of Rita?'

Jensa crossed one long leg over the other, leaned back against the desk and said clearly, 'She's stunningly beautiful, obviously high-spirited, and I'm sure, from your point of view, a great deal of fun. Accurate?'

'Entirely. Rita Mendez is a real woman.'

'And I'm not, I suppose.'

'That's your interpretation,' he said. 'However, if you feel guilty....'

'Not on your life! But I suppose I should be grateful

to her for fascinating you so. It relieves the rest of us from the bother of dealing with the likes of you.'

The small sense of triumph she felt seemed oddly hollow. Indulging in this sort of hurtful sparring had been totally outside Jensa's experience before she met Adam.

'Look,' she began, 'perhaps I am being unfair. I'm sure Rita has many fine qualities that I didn't have a chance to see on so short a meeting.'

'You're right there. I've had much more time in which to get to know her many talents.'

Jensa pulled a face of disgust and turned her back firmly on him. Flicking her fall of hair over her shoulders, she began with slow deliberation to trace the outline of a tissue section on the paper before her.

'Oh, dear ... Miss Welles has been shocked again,' he observed.

'Not at all. I do have eyes,' she replied coldly. 'But your friends and values are strictly your own business. I have no right to make judgments about them. I really couldn't care less, anyway.'

He came over to her side and leaned lazily on her desk. 'I'm glad to hear you say that. You're going to be spending more time in Rita's company soon, and it would be helpful if you could control your habit of making value judgments.'

'You mean she makes a habit of popping in on you out here just to check on your welfare?'

'No ... the station is a bit primitive for someone of Rita's tastes. But she's invited me to the Rancho Rosada for dinner two days from now. And you'll be going with me.'

'That is one pleasure, thank you very much, that I believe I will forgo. It would only take time away from my work, and being a third wheel has never been fun.'

'True. But in this case I think you'll find your time adequately occupied by Señor Mendez. He likes to be kept up to date on what's going on down here!'

'But why on earth should *I* go . . . surely you're much better qualified than I to fill him in on the work!'

He reached over imperiously and took the pen from Jensa's hand. Then, taking both her slender shoulders in his hands, he turned her around on the stool until she was facing him. He stared down at her with hard eyes, his manner suddenly very serious.

'I suspect,' he said, 'that Felipe is more interested in any publicity that may come his way out of this project than he is in the survival of these whales. It's vitally important that he should not lost interest in what's going on down here! Your drawings could prove more valuable than anything else in helping him to understand the importance of this work!'

'Then of course—if you put it that way—I'd be glad to take the drawings to him. I'll do whatever I can!'

He inhaled deeply and released her from his bruising grip. 'Fine, then. Use your charm on the old man—you do have a little feminine charm stashed away for emergencies, don't you? Felipe has been a widower for years, and it's well known that he has a fondness for young women. Your pale blonde looks could devastate him!'

Jensa set her delicate but stubborn jaw for battle. 'Oh, now look,' she blazed, 'I'll be delighted to try to impress the man with the urgency of what's going on here—but not in the distasteful way I have a sinking feeling *you're* talking about! My work will speak for itself. I'm not going to flutter my eyelashes at some ageing Lothario in order to win his approval!' Her tone was deliberately scathing.

He folded his arms across his chest and the voice

stiffened. 'You never stop fighting, do you ... have it your way then. Perhaps you're at your most charming when you're trying the least ... like right now, and you have those two little spots of red on your cheekbones that you always get when you decide to take me on.' He reached out and brushed the side of her cheek.

Jensa made a small noise of exasperation and roughly flicked his hand aside.

A hint of a smile played at the corners of his mouth. 'But you'll do it for the whales, won't you? No matter what you think of me.'

She threw him a contemptuous look. 'Yes,' she replied. 'For the whales. And strictly on my own terms.'

'I leave it to your fine judgment,' he said, and went to his desk whistling.

CHAPTER FOUR

IT was an impressive night's work. Jensa surveyed the orderly pile of drawings and allowed herself a smile of satisfaction. They had both worked, he in his tower, she at her desk, well into the morning. The elements had been unleashed again during the night, and sleep had eluded her. The windows rattled and the sand hit them with a noise like hail. But it had been oddly calming to sit at her desk, encircled by the warm pink glow of the oil lamp.

'I touched up some of the quick sketches I did of the breaching,' she said, 'thought it would save time.'

He was sitting scrunched up on the old sofa, his legs looking absurdly long. He nodded his approval. 'Then

you think you'll have a good cross-section done on time
—we'll leave just after lunch tomorrow.'

She tugged absently on the end of a long braid. 'No
problem ... if I go without another night's sleep.'

'Boy, do you make me sound like an ogre! I think I
better do something to improve my image around here.
Why don't you give it a break? Seriously—you're way
ahead of schedule, and you'll ruin your eyes if you stay
hunched up over that desk any longer.'

'I think you're right,' she said, smiling ruefully. 'I
see the sun's broken through ... if you really don't
mind, then, I think I'll take a good long walk.'

'I've got a better idea. Why don't we go up the coast
to the penguin and seal rookeries? It would be a damn
shame to come all this distance and not see them.'

Jensa's hard-won aloofness evaporated, and she was
off her seat with a most undignified bounce. 'Oh, we
couldn't—could we?'

'I think we might manage it,' he replied easily. He
untangled his legs and rose. 'Dress warmly, now. I'll
go and ask Maria if she'll pack us a lunch. It's a rough
drive up to Peninsula Valdes and it'll be evening before
we make it back.'

'I won't be five minutes!' said Jensa, grabbing her
tote bag and rummaging among her things on the desk.

'What's this all about—I thought you were going to
get dressed!'

'I will, I will ... don't be so impatient. I just want to
take some sketching equipment.' She tossed pens and
pencils and a dozen other things into the bag.

'The whole idea of this was to give you a break from
work!'

'This isn't work, silly,' she said indignantly. 'This is
fun!' She turned around and looked at him, laughing.

'Go on—I won't be late, I promise!'

The trip *will* be rough, she thought, biting her lip. She'd give anything if the Rover just had sides! So the jeans stayed on. But an impulse swept over her, and she quickly stripped off the coarse wool sweater. Shivering in her little wisp of a bra, she pulled her only good sweater out of her bag and slipped it on. It was a soft heather cashmere—a foolish thing to have packed for here, but at the time she simply hadn't thought.

She shook her hair out of its braids and brushed it till it shone. Then, half annoyed with herself for bothering, she applied a flick of mascara to her sweep of lashes and a smoothing of pale gloss on her lips.

With the soft wool poncho draped over her shoulders and a gay scarf tucked into her bag, she studied herself as best she could in the worn silvered mirror that hung in the alcove. She felt pleased—and somehow very festive. Almost as if she were heading to the smartest restaurant in Montreal rather than to some rock-strewn beach.

Montreal, she thought. Restaurants ... and Ross! With a stab of guilt she pulled open her bag. Yes, it was still there ... the postcard she had written to him on the airplane and meant to mail in Puerto Madryn. But not since she'd stepped off the plane had thoughts of Ross MacLean crossed her mind.

She *had* tried to contact him before she left, she tried to comfort herself. But he'd been in surgery. She had stood beside Ross in surgery herself, and knew just how good he was. He had been the resident assisting on the child's facial surgery she had illustrated.

It wasn't that she owed Ross an explanation of her comings and goings, she thought, a tiny frown line forming on her brow. They'd had no more than a few dates. But he was nice, and she didn't want to appear cold to him.

She smiled as she remembered her last evening out with the fair-haired young doctor. They had gone to a play put on by one of the city's small experimental groups. After that, it was on to a favourite bistro where they had sat well into the morning over plates of pâté and crusty bread and large glasses of good wine.

It had been pleasant with Ross, those few evenings ... fun, relaxed. Ross had made no attempt to hide the fact that he had found Jensa a very attractive companion, but he hadn't pushed. There had been passion in his last kiss. But it was controlled, gentle, not like——

Adam, she thought. He'd have the Rover in front of the house by now. She grabbed her things, and leaving the postcard forgotten on the bed, hurried out of the door and down the steps to the waiting car.

It was with the help of Adam's eyes, on the teeth-rattling ride up to Peninsula Valdes, that the vast expanse of beige desert came alive to Jensa. Without his expertise, she would have missed most of the unique wildlife, so skilfully had nature hidden it in its fierce and inhospitable homeland.

'Only the tough, conservative forms make it here,' he explained, skilfully easing the car over the vaguely defined road. 'They don't go in for the elaborate plumage and pelts you see in other parts of the world. But while the colours may be dull, the actual life forms are just fantastic.'

What there was of the road finally petered out and the land became too rugged even for the Rover. Adam parked it in the shelter of a shelf of rock. He stuffed their lunch and a tattered blanket into a knapsack which he slung on to his back, then struck out briskly in the direction of the ocean, with Jensa following up the rear, toting her sketch pad and shoulder-bag.

A few yards down the path, he stopped and crouched to Jensa's level. With one hand resting on her shoulder, the other stretched out in front of her, he indicated a comical procession ahead of them.

'Cavies,' he whispered. A small, rabbit-like creature on high, stiff legs, with the bobbing line of her babies trailing after her, cut across a patch of desert and disappeared down a burrow.

'The last time I was here I spotted a pool not far down the path,' he went on. 'With luck, we might spot something else interesting.'

They were not disappointed. Five minutes later, Adam gestured to her to crouch down behind him. Creeping up to a large outcropping of rock, they peered down into a tiny waterhole. Small brown Patagonian ducks darted over the surface of the pond while rare Darwin rheas—ostrich-like birds—calmly strutted at the edge of the water and stopped to take long sips.

Where the land began to taper and thrust out into the surging, grey Atlantic, the cliffs were black with the bodies of cormorants and the air alive with their raucous chattering. The birds reeled and spun high overhead in the treacherous wind, their mouths trailing long banners of seaweed for their nests.

Jensa kept herself squarely behind Adam's broad back in an effort to hide from him the fact that her breath was now coming to her in laboured little puffs.

It was a futile ploy, however, and she noticed that he had begun to slacken his pace to accommodate her tinier step. Occasionally, he wordlessly slipped strong hands under her elbows when she came to a particularly intimidating rock, causing her pulse to quicken.

'Not much farther,' he said bracingly. 'Looks like a penguin rookery just over there—half a mile more should do it, then we'll take a break.'

Jensa groaned inwardly. She had thought herself in condition, but the miles of pebbles were beginning to make unwanted impressions on the soles of her hiking boots. While her thigh muscles screamed for relief, she trudged doggedly on, shifting her sketching equipment —which she almost regretted bringing—from one aching arm to the other.

Her first sight of the Magellanic penguins swept that regret away. Thousands of the comic, friendly little creatures swarmed over the shore, some waddling right up to the two human intruders. They were so funny on land, strutting like Lilliputian generals. But when they approached the precipice and plunged heart-stoppingly into the frigid waters, they suddenly came into their own. Completely forgetting Adam, Jensa clapped in delight as they shed their clumsiness and shot up out of the waves in graceful arcs.

They scrambled deeper into the mass of speckled bodies. 'Look at the little ones, Adam,' she laughed, 'so waif-like and bedraggled!' She spotted one fledgling struggling in a tidal pool and bent to rescue it.

'Still got his fluff,' Adam explained as she cooed over it. 'Until he sheds it, he'll be as helpless as a kitten in the water.'

'They're so trusting,' she said, taking up her pencil. 'Don't they have any natural fears at all?'

'Not too many, unfortunately for them. In the heyday of the whalers, even *they* came in for it—walked right up to the fat rendering pots like lambs to the slaughter. They were just tossed right in.'

It was far too soon for Jensa when Adam stood. 'Better be heading on,' he said crisply. 'But don't worry—it's worth it,' he added, noting Jensa's wince. Wordlessly, he took her bag of equipment and added it to his own load. Jensa hesitated, wondering if she should insist on carrying her share. But she considered the impressions made by the bag handle on her wind-nipped fingers and settled for a quick smile of appreciation.

As they struck out farther into the peninsula, she suddenly felt her first apprehension. They were so exposed, so vulnerable. She remembered the violence of the storm that had battered the research station. If it happened again, where on earth would they find shelter out here?

And then there was Adam himself. So far, he had been restrained, almost friendly. But she knew, painfully, the unpredictable nature of the man, and she had not forgotten the forcefulness of his kiss that first night. She was suddenly very aware of the fact that in all the miles they had travelled, they had not seen a single human being.

Glancing up at Adam secretly, she saw his profile outlined against the iron sky. They're well matched, she thought, this man and this land. Both hard and unforgiving. Both ravished by storms. She studied the cleanly defined face, the relentless persistence of the striding body. What is the storm that rages inside you, Adam? she wondered. She'd never know. And that was just as well.

They rounded the bend in the cliff and struggled the last few yards to the top of the promontory that gave a sweeping view of the tip of the peninsula where it thrust its farthest into the Atlantic. Jensa was struck speechless by the sight laid out before her. It was awesome, humbling, and infinitely exciting.

The barren land where odd forms of life scratched for survival met abruptly with an ocean which teemed with life thriving in the vast Atlantic plankton beds. Seaward, whales swam in lazy circles and dusky dolphins frolicked above the waves. Overhead, gulls and cormorants wheeled and screamed. And below, on the sand, were the creatures that spanned both worlds.

Here was the breeding ground of the world's greatest colony of sea-lions. Thousands of them paved the shore thickly with a heaving, quivering mass of flesh. Jensa trembled without apology as she watched in awe.

Above the general din of braying animals and shrieking birds rose the air-rending roar of a regal bull lion.

'Ah,' cried Adam, pointing him out to Jensa, 'the patriarch calls his wives around him—good man!' Far below her, she could see the maned neck of the bull, a dark, undulating pile of almost a ton, surrounded by his harem of females. Here and there, dotting the great mounds of flesh, were the small furry bodies of the pups, barking sharply and slithering around awkwardly. Jensa could not imagine how the mothers kept track of their young, or the bulls of their wives. But, given the enormity of the breeding colony, nature apparently made its arrangements rather well.

'How much farther down can we go?' she asked, secretly dying to hold one of the fuzzy little pups.

'Not any.' His reply was firm. 'These aren't toys—they're animals on their own territory. I can't afford to have you turned into a pancake by some outraged bull just because you think his son is adorable! We'll picnic

here,' he added, indicating the slight shelter of an inclined rock. 'Close enough for you to sketch in safety,
and high enough for me to get in a little whale sight-
ing.'

Jensa set to work at once, her head bent over her
pad, her hair falling in soft tendrils about her wind-
reddened cheeks. Adam smoked his pipe in silence,
knees bent and feet planted wide, his face tipped up to
the weak rays of the sun. From time to time he peered
through the small but powerful binoculars he produced from his knapsack, and jotted down notes in the
pocket diary that was always with him.

'It's not so different from any *human* public beach,
is it?' mused Jensa. 'The mothers trying to doze, the
children obviously with other ideas.' She pointed to
where a pup frisked over his napping mother until,
exasperated, she gave her high-spirited offspring a
gentle cuff. The chastised baby shuffled off to look for
more co-operative playmates.

Adam rummaged in the knapsack and produced
Maria's lunch—crusty sandwiches of Argentinian
corned beef, cheese, a sweet. 'Hungry?' he asked, passing her some.

'Famished,' she confessed. 'And freezing.'

'This should help,' he said, pulling a second, smaller
thermos from the bag. 'I don't usually keep things like
this around the station, but I happened to pick up a
bottle when I was in Puerto Madryn. Had it in mind
that Josh and I could drink to old times.'

'Lovely,' said Jensa, inhaling the rich, heady fragrance of the wine. She sipped it appreciatively, feeling
it warm her. She knew enough about wine to know that
the one Adam had brought was a good one.

'You appreciate wine,' he said, eyeing her sharply
across his cup.

'I do,' she agreed. 'Although I'm not much interested in anything stronger.'

'Tell me about it—home, friends, family,' he said unexpectedly.

Her mood softened by the wine, she complied. 'Home is a floor in an old grey stone house in the centre of Montreal. Tiny, ancient—but charming. It must have been elegant in its day. It's still pretty nice—but given to the ailments of the very old.'

'Such as?'

'Well ... the furnace is very cranky, prone to conking out on the worst night of the year. The windows are draughty and the water pipes clank and complain a good deal. My kitchen is actually a closet in disguise.'

'But I suspect you love it,' he said. 'And if someone miraculously offered you a penthouse apartment in a glass skyscraper, with every known convenience, you'd probably look faintly regretful—and say no.'

She laid her head back against the boulder. 'Absolutely. Look at the compensations—soaring ceilings, carved mouldings, fabulously elegant windows ... and a marble fireplace that actually works!'

'And is vital a good deal of the winter,' he added dryly.

'True,' she admitted. 'But nothing could be cosier. My living-room overlooks the street, and you can't imagine a lovelier sight on a winter's day than the snow drifting down silently, the only noise the sputtering of the fire.'

'An inviting picture,' he said, reaching across her to refill her cup. 'And with whom do you share these idyllic moments—anyone special?'

'Not yet,' she replied easily. She thought again, and not without some inexplicable guilt, of Ross. There were others, of course. Artists, the publishers of the nature books she'd illustrated, a reporter who'd once interviewed her about her work. No, there was no lack of invitations ... dinners at Montreal's excellent French restaurants, ski excursions to the Laurentians. But there'd been no one, yet, who'd held any claim on her.

Perhaps, she mused, sipping the wine, she'd been too protective of her independence. It had been so hard-won because of her parents' fears for her. Or perhaps she'd set her standards too high. A lot of the men she dated would qualify as good husbands. But nagging at the back of her mind was the thought that, despite all her surface sophistication, she was clinging to the schoolgirl notion that she should experience that spark —that quick stab to her heart that romance was supposed to bring.

'—Jensa?'

She started and looked up. Adam's eyes were boring into her.

'I suspect I've stirred up all sorts of memories,' he said.

'A few,' she confessed.

'And how does your family feel about your career?'

'Not terribly happy,' she said, giving a rueful smile. 'Thought I ought to do something more practical.'

'Such as?'

'Getting married,' she answered, pulling a face.

'I'm sure you could have pulled that off with ease, but I suspect you had your sights set higher.'

'Not higher,' she insisted. 'Just in a different direction for a while. My parents have known difficult times,' she explained, struggling to be fair. 'It's made them terribly conservative. When I went off to the city to study, and moved in with Josh and Evie....' She paused and pressed her lips together, feeling again a not quite forgotten pain. 'Well, let's just say there was some unpleasantness. But that's past history now.' She smiled up at him gamely.

'Surely they're proud of your success now? You must make quite a decent living.'

'I manage very well. There's not much profit in some of the little books I've illustrated—not enough demand for things like an illustrated guide to lichen in the Quebec woods! But I do them because they deserve to be published. Things like the medical journal pay enough to compensate.'

'How did you get into that—Josh?'

'No, by accident, really, through a book I'd done on herb gardens. It was a charming little thing—filled with snippets of history, remembrances, recipes. Anyway, I did several illustrations of gardens, a few with children in them studying the plants, playing on the brick paths, that sort of thing. They were, of necessity, very delicate, precise drawings. The author's husband saw them—he's a plastic surgeon. He liked the style ... thought it was just what he wanted to illustrate an article he was doing on reconstructing a child's face who'd been badly burned. It meant taking a crash course in anatomy, but I wanted to have a go at it.'

'Squeamish?'

'Terribly, at first. But what can you do?'

'Faint, I should think.'

'Frowned upon, for some strange reason,' she replied, 'by all those very stern scrub nurses.'

Dark clouds began to crowd in on the sky, casting a peculiar violet light over them. Jensa drew her hands under the poncho and hugged herself. Shaking her head, she declined his offer of the last of the wine, and watched as he drained it into his mug.

'I'm surprised that someone who lives in such primitive surroundings has a knowledge of the complexities of choosing good wine,' she commented.

He gave a short, not very pleasant laugh. 'I haven't always lived like this,' he replied. 'In fact, wine was an everyday thing in our home when I was growing up, along with good food, books, music. My father appreciated these things and made a point of teaching me.'

'Was he a very social man, then, Adam?' Jensa asked.

'Not at all. He was very much dedicated to his work. He was a marine biologist too, by the way. My mother was bored to death by it.'

'I suspect many wives might share her feelings about such a remote field—but surely she had her hands full raising you!'

He gave a short laugh. 'She found child-rearing about as interesting as one of my father's conversations about photoplankton. One day she packed her bags, gave me a dry little kiss on the cheek and said she was going on a trip. She never came back. She went to live in New York. From what I used to read in the society pages when I got older, she got what she wanted finally—a constant round of parties and the frivolity that passes for living among the idle rich.'

'It must have been a great comfort to your father to have a son who shared his love of science,' Jensa offered.

'That came much later, of course,' he replied, roughly tearing a chunk of bread off the loaf. 'He was gone for months at a time on sea expeditions. I was left to the not so tender mercies of various boarding schools.' He tossed a scrap of bread out to a rock where a red-eyed cormorant hovered, waiting cannily for hand-outs.

'Gradually it came to me,' he continued, 'that if I was going to get any attention at all from my father, I was going to have to share his work. We did finally share a certain closeness—but not until I was almost an adult. He died a few years ago. I don't think he ever really understood, even at the end, just how painful things had been when I was growing up. Perhaps he was too hurt himself and I was just a reminder of that pain. At any rate,' he said, shrugging, 'we finally reached some sort of understanding. Whatever his weaknesses as a father, he did give me the one thing that matters in my life—my love of science, of animals.'

'And your mother?' asked Jensa quietly. 'Did you ever reach an understanding with her?'

He slouched back against the rock and raised the binoculars to his eyes as he spoke. 'I saw her only once after she deserted us. I was already in my twenties and in New York for a seminar on sea law, and I looked her up. It was a mistake,' he said coldly.

'Oh, surely not, Adam?' she protested. 'You had to make the effort!'

'Perhaps. But there wasn't much doubt, from her point of view, that it was a wasted effort on my part. She did make time for me, however, between luncheon and dinner engagements. It's funny,' he said, 'but I remembered her as young and beautiful and laughing. I guess all little boys see their mothers that way. It was stupid —but I hadn't prepared myself for the ageing. She was old and too thin and wore too much make-up. I remember how it caked and ran into deep lines around her mouth. There were smudges of mascara under her eyes.'

Jensa shivered again and stared out across the ocean, wishing suddenly that she hadn't encouraged this raw and ugly exposure of private memories.

She heard herself say gently, 'That meeting must have been very painful for her, Adam. Did you give her a chance?'

'All she deserved. What chance did she give her six-year-old son?'

'Then she's to be pitied Adam—not condemned!' Listen to me, she thought a little wildly, lecturing him! How reckless can I get!

He looked hard at her, his mouth cruel. 'She was a great beauty in her day,' he said slowly. 'Just like you, Jensa.'

Something tightened painfully in her chest, but she would not back down. 'I suppose you're implying that any woman who has been gifted by God with looks is doomed to be heartless, self-centred and loose!' she said sharply. 'If you have such disdain for women in general—and beautiful women in particular—how is it that you find someone like Rita Mendez so appealing and trustworthy?'

'Trust doesn't enter into it. Rita is appealing because she's honest. She doesn't pretend to be anything other that what she is—a ravishing young woman who's a great deal of fun to be around. And she is not, may I add, given to preaching at me in pious tones.'

'All right,' said Jensa, plunking her cup down on the blanket, 'I can see there's no arguing with you—but I still say you should confine yourself to analysing *animal* behaviour.'

'I certainly *prefer* to confine myself to animal be-haviour,' he retorted, snapping a match with his thumbnail and lighting his pipe. 'Whales make very devoted mothers—did I tell you that? Whalers used to take advantage of that ... they'd often attack the slower-moving calf, knowing full well its cries of agony would make the mother stay by its side, frantic with concern. They they'd close in on the mother.'

They were back on safe ground, she thought, watching him. His face had changed somehow. It was closed, blank. He hadn't told her about his parents because he felt comfortable with her or needed to confide in someone. More likely, he had only been trying to put her down again. Perhaps if she'd been older, or less attractive, she'd have met with a more civil response from him at the Puerto Madryn airport. If she really did remind him of his mother, how he must loathe her presence at the station and be counting the days till she would leave!

She felt chilled to the marrow and quickly followed his lead to a safer topic. 'You said before that these whales were making a comeback from near extinction, Adam—are they still endangered?'

'Absolutely. That's why it's so desperately important that we get this material pulled together on schedule. It'll be published in book form later on, of course, but much of it I'll be presenting at an international conference on whaling that's coming up next month in Buenos Aires. What happens there may well decide the future of these whales.'

Jensa tucked her legs under her, tailor-fashion, and rested her elbows on them as she faced him. 'What is it that you're hoping for?'

'We've *got* to get international approval for more protection of this area as a breeding ground.'

'And what about Señor Mendez—where does he fit into all this?'

'Right smack in the middle. It's not enough to have ocean protection—you've got to have it on the land side as well. This whole area where we are now,' said Adam, sweeping his arm around behind her, 'has been already designated a national wildlife preserve. There are several Argentinian and international scientists working here now. This is what we need down where we are!' Jensa watched the large, veined hands cutting through the air, underlining each word, emphasising the urgency of his message. 'There's no time for the usual red tape that hamstrings most of these commissions,' he explained.

'You must have talked to Señor Mendez about the land already—how does he feel about it?'

'I just don't know yet,' he replied, for the first time sounding the slightest bit weary. 'He's a guarded man. He indicated an interest in maintaining ownership of the land but agreeing to create a sanctuary on it.'

'That would be a solution, wouldn't it?'

He slapped a fist against a palm. 'Somehow I don't see it working out. It would mean leaving himself open to a certain amount of interference from various authorities. Felipe's not the type of man to tolerate anyone telling him what to do.'

'Couldn't things just go on as they are? After all, you said that the land's not being used any more for ranching.'

Adam pressed his lips together and shook his head. 'No, it's only a matter of time before something happens to endanger those whales. It may not be this month, or even this year, but it always comes. If they've to have any kind of a shot at survival, we've got to get that area established as a sanctuary now ... legally and irrevocably.'

'And what about Rita?' asked Jensa cautiously. 'Does she have any influence with her father?'

'Some. But I'm not deliberately cultivating her company in the hopes that she'll put in a good word for me with papa, if that's what's going through that devious mind of yours, Jensa.'

'Not at all,' she replied. Adam Ryder wasn't the sort to be shy about the things that matter to him! she thought.

At that moment there was a thunderous explosion seaward, and Jensa's head shot up just in time to see a burst of foam break the surface of the Atlantic. A sea-lion shot violently into the air. Moments later, a shiny black whale, different from the ones at the station, breached. As the sea-lion fell back to the water, it opened its sharp, tooth-edged jaws. In seconds it had grabbed the helpless sea-lion and pulled it beneath the waves.

Jensa turned questioningly to Adam, with eyes that were wide with shock.

'Killer whale,' he said. 'They sometimes hunt in packs around here.'

'How cruel life is,' Jensa said, shuddering involuntarily.

'Yes,' he agreed, 'it is.' He turned and looked at her, then became suddenly brisk. 'It's upset you, I see. Well, that wind's rising and I think we'd better head back.'

She was glad to go. The wind was beginning to penetrate her clothes with its rawness, and their shelter behind the ledge of rock now seemed pitifully inadequate. Quickly and silently, they repacked their gear and returned to the Rover as rapidly as the rocky landscape permitted them.

Doing things, such as washing, that had been simple

and pleasurable back in her Montreal flat now required great ingenuity. She had succeeded, after much hauling and boiling of water, in ridding herself of several layers of Patagonian sand. She sat now, wrapped in her robe, her hair freshly washed, skin glowing, innocent of make-up.

'Maria—I didn't expect to see you back here this late!'

The small bundled figure braced herself against the resisting door and pushed it shut. 'I always make a fresh thermos of coffee for Dr Ryder when he spends all night on the beach recording. Every time he tells me not to bother, and every time I do it anyway,' Maria laughed. She busied herself cheerfully at the little propane stove.

'You mean he won't be back all night?'

'Probably not. José tells me there was much activity out there while you were up at Peninsula Valdes today.'

'Does he often stay out like that?' asked Jensa.

'Oh yes. Sometimes he goes for days with only little naps ... he is a very fine scientist!' Maria beamed as she spoke. Neither she nor José had made any secret to Jensa of their affection and respect for their employer.

Into a small straw bag, Maria put the coffee, a small loaf of bread, and a wedge of cheese. 'The only thing I don't like,' she said, 'is the walk to the beach—it is so dark out there tonight!'

'Why don't you let me take that down, Maria?' Jensa asked, understanding the woman's reluctance to walk out to the water.

'Oh, I couldn't ask you to do that for me, Miss Welles!'

'You're not,' said Jensa reassuringly. 'Off with you, and don't give it another thought!'

She smiled brightly at a relieved Maria.

The voluminous poncho would more than cover her nightgown. She pulled it on over her head, slipped her feet into sneakers, and at the last minute remembered the spare flashlight hanging from a hook by the door.

She needed that light—it wasn't until you got out into complete wilderness like this, she told herself, that you realised just how dark the night can be. The beach was reached, however, without loss of limb or thermos, and she turned to follow the shoreline to where she guessed Adam was set up. She had gone only a few hesitant steps when she heard him call out.

'Maria? Still ignoring my orders, I see! Stay where you are . . . I'll come and fetch the thermos!'

'It's me, Adam . . . Jensa. I thought I'd save Maria the trip—I can see now why she dislikes it so!'

Footsteps came nearer and she saw his shadowy shape emerge from the darkness into the pale light of the moon. 'I hope you don't mind,' she said, looking up into a face still hidden in shadow.

He was silent, then she felt his hands touch her arms and draw her gently forward towards the flickering circle of gold light that marked his encampment. Close to, where the water washed over the pebbled beach with a silvery noise, lay a campfire. Beside it, a dish-shaped receiver pointed towards the Atlantic. A battery of complex recording devices lay around it.

'The natives are restless tonight,' he said wryly. 'I've been getting some terrific recordings.'

'What will you do with them?' she asked, squinting at the array of dials and screens that glowed with a pale green light.

'Try and correlate them with activities we've observed. A lot of the data is coded and fed into the computer—it's a great help in picking up patterns that we might overlook.' He looked at her more closely. 'You'll catch cold sitting—come over here on the blanket next to the fire.' Jensa was feeling the raw cold of the salt air too much to bridle at his authoritative manner this time. Quickly she lowered herself on to the blanket and rubbed her hands over the delicious warmth of the fire. Adam crouched beside her, laying his sleeping bag over both of them.

'Coffee?' he asked.

'Please ... except there's only one mug. I didn't think to bring an extra.'

'You'll survive sharing one with me, I should think. I don't feel myself coming down with any rare and deadly disease.'

She accepted the mug from his outstretched hand and sipped from it, feeling warmth revive her. She watched silently as Adam adjusted dials, the earphones pressed down over a shock of thick, wind-blown hair. He was lost in concentration, his eyes focused somewhere in the darkness before him. Finally he yanked off the earphones with a smile of triumph.

'It's first-rate tonight!' he said. 'Here—see what you can make of it.' Before Jensa could move, he had pulled off her cap and set the phones on her head. She shivered, feeling his fingers brush lightly against her ears as he pushed back the strands of hair which fell about her shoulders.

She closed her eyes and pressed her fingertips against her temples, trying to sort out the jumble of whistles and crackles that came through the headpiece.

She shook her head. 'No ... I don't think——'

Join the Mills & Boon Reader Service and get much, much more, for a great deal less.

TAKE 2 BOOKS FREE EVERY MONTH

Turn the page for more exciting benefits!

'Quiet!' he admonished her. 'Just wait ... concentrate!' Gradually, some sort of order did start to reveal itself to her. She glanced quickly up at Adam whose eyes were fastened on her face, and smiled her excitement and comprehension to him.

'I can hear all kinds of swishes and background noises, of course. But there's a deeper noise ... like moaning.'

'I'm pretty sure that what we've had out there today is a female and two males,' he told her.

They pressed their heads together, both straining to hear the rhythmic rise and fall of the deep, haunting noise. At one point the great smooth back of one of the whales broke the surface of the cove, scattering a silver shower of phosphorescence behind it.

Jensa sat electrified by the sight of the slowly circling animal. 'There's emotion there, and intelligence,' she said at last.

'Yes,' he agreed quietly. 'Those aren't indiscriminate sounds—they have meaning, intensity.'

'What are they doing?' she asked, setting down the phones and turning to look at him. The strong lines of his face were mottled with amber from the leaping flames.

'Before, I think we had two suitors pressing their cases with a female—there are love triangles in the animal world too, you know. By the sound of things now, however, I'd wager the issue has been resolved.'

'You mean they're mating, then?'

'Uh-huh. We humans like to think that the higher emotions are reserved for us, but I have no doubt that these whales are quite capable of very deep emotion. Love, if you will. I've watched while the male circles the female, touching her the length of her body while she lolls in the water above him. They roll against each other—their bodies ripple as they do it. I'm sure it gives them erotic pleasure. It's not at all unlike a human man and woman caressing each other.'

Jensa felt a flush spread across her breast at the explicitness of his words. It was not that he had intended to be crude—quite the opposite, she was sure. As usual, when he was speaking about his whales, his voice mellowed and was full of compassion and humanity. She was oddly stirred by it.

She felt his breath on her cheek as he bent to listen in with her. Her shoulder tingled where the breadth of his chest pressed against her. She brought her concentration sharply back to what he was trying to explain to her.

'She's probably been floating belly up during all this—letting him stroke her, but keeping herself out of position for mating. When she rolls over to breathe, he'll quickly get into proper alignment with her before she gets another chance to outmanoeuvre him.'

Jensa knitted her brow with an effort to keep her mind firmly on his words, on the dials and charts, but it was no use. This was not a time when words and ideas held any claim on her. The low, erotic moans that came from the sea, the rhythmic slapping of the waves on the shore, the presence of this powerful man so close to her, shook her with a frightening intensity.

Get hold of yourself, she lectured herself silently. You're not entirely naïve.

She was only too aware that despite her dislike of casual involvements with men, she had her own healthy instincts. But she had always tried to keep a sensible rein on her emotions, and had put off any man who had threatened to overwhelm her natural reserve.

She knew physical passion, but it had never ruled her. This was different. Here, on this deserted beach of time-worn pebbles, a place that spoke of primeval forces and things beyond human control, she felt her nerves bared before Adam. She struggled desperately to say something technical and matter-of-fact that would shatter the eroticism of the moment. But the mood that gripped her kept her mute.

The raw wind of the Argentinian winter cut through her poncho and sent a shiver the length of her. Suddenly she knew she had to get away, be anywhere except beside Adam Ryder on this forsaken beach.

A hand shot out and gripped her wrist like a band of steel. 'You're going?'

'Yes ... I'm freezing. I should have dressed more warmly before I came, but I never intended to stay this long.'

He reached down and fingered the silky fabric of her nightgown that edged out from beneath the poncho. 'Yes, it was rather foolish to come down so scantily dressed.'

'Really, Adam,' she protested weakly, 'I'm perishing from the cold——'

Roughly, he enclosed her in the sleeping bag. As he did, one hand accidentally brushed aside the wool cloak and caught the gentle curve of her waist covered only by her tissuey gown. He held her firmly there beside him while he stirred the fire.

The sudden flash of heat and light as the embers flared into flames was not unlike the sensation that shot through Jensa at the touch of his hand so close to her flesh. She trembled and damned her body for its treachery. Why did it have to happen every time they were close, this demanding, consuming desire!

'It's no good—I've got to go,' she pleaded. But it was too late. A shudder went through her body, and it was excitement, not cold, that was its source. One of his hands held her jaw while the other, that had claimed her waist, slipped up her back and pinned her to him.

'I'll warm you, Jensa,' he murmured in her ear as his lips slid lightly down her neck until they hungrily claimed the pulsing spot at its base. A soft moan of pleasure escaped from her lips and he tightened his grip on her body.

What was left of rational thought urged her to reject him, but she could not. For long moments, the sound of their own pleasure mingled with those rising from the sea. With one strong move Adam pressed her unprotesting body against the sand and covered it with his. His mouth opened hers searchingly and she did not disappoint him. She felt herself arch against him.

But when his hands found the soft curve of her breast at the top of her gown and she heard the urgency in his breathing, sanity at last returned to her. She realised that her struggles against him now must seem indistinguishable from her passion of a few moments before. In desperation, she pressed her nails into his face and heard his gasp of pain.

'What's this?' he rasped into her ear, his fingers threatening to crush her slender wrists. 'You're not asking me to stop now, are you? Not after the way you've returned my lovemaking!'

'Yes ... yes. That's exactly what I'm asking. And if you've any decency in you at all, Adam, you'll let me go now,' she pleaded in a trembling voice.

'Why should I?' he mocked her. 'You kiss very well, you know. You've acted like such a snow queen ever since you got here—but now I know what lies beneath that cool façade!'

'Please, Adam,' she begged. 'I was attracted to you— I don't deny that. But you can see that it must stop now!'

'I only see that you want me as much as I want you.'

'That's not true,' she protested. 'Not now!'

'What was it, then?' he demanded, looking down at her with a gaze so dark and glinting that she felt dizzy.

'It ... it was this place ... this atmosphere. I don't know—but you've got to let go of me or——'

'Or you'll what, my dear?' he challenged in a voice that was hard and disdainful.

'I'll scream,' she said. 'And Maria and José will come—and then what will they think of the wonderful Dr Ryder?' she threw out wildly. She knew her desperation must have sounded ridiculously melodramatic to him, and felt a wave of sickening humiliation when she saw him throw back his head and laugh harshly.

Suddenly he released her from his grip with a flicking, impatient gesture, as if ridding himself of something particularly distasteful. 'Run along to bed, Jensa, I've no need to force a woman to get what I want. You'll be quite safe now.'

She saw the coldness in his eyes and felt something die inside her. This casual rejection of her after the insatiable demands of his kisses was devastating— almost as devastating as it would have been if he had insisted on taking her.

He was brushing sand off his pants, his face utterly impassive. It was as if nothing had happened between them. She had the release she had begged, but the words she wanted to hurl at him died in her throat and still she could not move.

'Well—go on with you,' he said, turning casually to the array of equipment. 'I've got a full night's work ahead of me. I don't have any more time to waste on adolescent hysterics.'

The casual cruelty of his words was like a lash across Jensa's heart. Silently she stumbled to her feet, confused and awkward and guilty. Guilty, she thought. How had he managed to make *her* feel that way? But she could not help but acknowledge the shame she felt for coming so close to succumbing to this man and his animal passions. She picked up the flashlight and began to pick her way along the path.

The last thing she heard as she struggled the last few feet to the top of the cliff was his mocking voice, whipped up to her on the wind. He was wishing her sweet dreams.

CHAPTER FIVE

'I DON'T suppose, Miss Welles, that you happened to bring a dinner dress with you.'

Jensa stopped her pen in mid-line. 'How very astute of you, Dr Ryder.'

'But you'll manage to look fairly presentable this afternoon, I hope.'

'When I arrived here, Adam,' she rapped out, 'you were jumping all over me because I didn't come equipped with clompy boots and bushwhacker's gear! And now I'm supposed to come up with a dinner dress?' She spun around on her stool and met the mocking look on her employer's face. She realised that

she had risen to the bait. He'd done it, she fumed ...
got her goat when she had tried to be so studiously cool
and professional all morning. 'Besides,' she added, trying to sound calm and dignified, 'I thought we were
going to a sheep ranch—how dressy could that be?'

'In this case, very. It's true that it's a sheep ranch—
thousands of the woolly little creatures dotting the landscape. Also oil rigs.'

'Ah ...' said Jensa, nodding, 'I'm beginning to get
the picture. I may assume, then, that there'll be
Spanish antiques and servants and such? And of course
your Rita, resplendent in the family jewels?'

'You've got it.'

'Well,' she replied, smiling thinly, 'Jensa Welles,
resplendent in practical wool travelling suit, will also
have to grace the Mendez mansion. I should feel quite
at home there with all those sheep. Take it or leave it.'

'As long as you have those smashing drawings tucked
under your tailored arm ... and a kind smile for Señor
Mendez on your usually grumpy face ... I suppose
I'll take it,' he replied.

Jensa returned to her work and sighed. She remembered the outfit Rita had worn on her visit and concluded grimly that the Argentinian girl would indeed
look positively gorgeous for the dinner.

She cast a sideways glance at her employer and felt
something alarmingly close to jealousy nip at her.
Shaking her head, she reminded herself sharply of his
unspeakable behaviour the night before. But she remembered, too, the exquisite tenderness of his mouth
against her cheek. She was forced to admit that she had
not been entirely successful in regretting the incident.

Jensa gasped and did a little dance from foot to foot as

the icy water splashed over her naked skin. She grabbed a towel and rubbed warmth back into her arms.

She thought about the huge, old-fashioned tub in her Montreal apartment, and the sheer animal pleasure of soaking in foaming, perfumed water. She'd done that the last time she'd prepared herself for a dinner date— with Ross. Ross, she thought. So different from Adam. A refined man with whom she had intimate, civilised little dinners in elegant restaurants. And Adam ... a brute of a man with whom she shared coarse sand-wiches on rock-littered beaches.

She hung her pants-suit on the curtain rod and brushed it vigorously, frowning as she worked. The comparison between the two men would not leave her mind. And yet ... she thought. No food had ever tasted so delicious to her than their picnics by the water. No silk gown had ever made her more aware of her woman's body than her jeans and coarse sweaters— with Adam's eyes on them.

She knew she was restless and tense. But how could she make herself feel better when she couldn't even decide what the problem was? The suit would be fine, she reassured herself. She'd be attractive in an under-stated—not flashy—way. She thought, a bit unkindly, of the picture of Rita in the red dress.

She squinted at the tiny mirror. Not bad, she judged. She brushed delicate tendrils of hair about her face and finished her face with a brighter-than-usual lipstick. She was touching her wrists with fragrance from a tiny gold tube when she heard Adam's heavy tread enter the room.

'Dressed, Cinderella?'

'One second!' she called.

She took a deep breath, one last look in the mirror,

and pulled back the curtain. She saw his eyes travelled knowingly from her head to her toe, but he said nothing.

'Well——?' she demanded finally, in exasperation. 'Will I do?'

The fine lines at the corners of his eyes crinkled slightly. He knocked the bowl of his pipe against the side of an ashtray. 'It's not silk or feathers,' he said slowly, 'but you'll do.'

Jensa slapped her comb and lipstick into her bag with angry little clicks. 'I can't imagine why I let myself be concerned about *my* appearance,' she muttered. 'You always look like a refugee from a coalmine!'

'Precisely why I'm here, Miss Welles. If you're all through in the alcove, my clothes are in there——'

'Be my guest,' she replied huffily. 'I'll get the drawings together while you try to rub off a few of the rough edges.'

Half an hour later, as she carefully slipped the last of the illustrations into a folder, she heard the curtain slide back and looked up. The papers remained suspended in mid-air for moments, until she remembered herself and returned to her job with forced deliberation.

Do *not*, she admonished herself silently, look up at him. Do *not* let him see that you think he's the most devastatingly handsome man for a thousand miles. His already swelled head would simply explode!

But her eyes were drawn to him irresistibly as he busied himself transferring car keys, pipe and wallet into his suit pocket. He had always seemed so barbaric and unrefined that she was totally unprepared for the smooth, sophisticated appearance he presented to her now.

The fawn suit was obviously hand-tailored, the way it curved at his slender waist and accommodated the broad shoulders with easy elegance. The brown face and sunbleached hair were startling against the snowy cotton shirt. She watched as the strong hands absently adjusted the muted silk tie.

He had always seemed so at ease in his work clothes, that she had never imagined him looking any different. She knew he had a past, of course—boarding schools, culture—privilege, even, if she were to judge from what he had told her at Peninsula Valdes. But that past had not seemed real to her—until now. It was all she could do to tear her eyes away.

Settled in her seat, the collar of her raincoat turned up high around her neck, she made a point of remaining as far away from him as possible. There was something about the well-tailored length of leg resting against the accelerator, the wrist lying relaxed over the top of the steering wheel, that unsettled her.

At length he turned to her and said, 'You're very silent . . . things on your mind?'

'Just Señor Mendez and how I'll approach him about the preserve,' she said evasively.

'Tell me what you've brought,' he ordered. 'Maybe I can give you a few pointers.'

'I included a few technical studies—I thought they'd look very official and impressive, you know? But not too many. I was afraid they might turn him off.'

'True.'

'Mostly I brought dramatic things—I thought they might give a layman a clearer picture of what it is we're trying to save.' She saw him nod in agreement. 'And I brought another series that I think—in all due modesty, of course . . .'

'Of course . . .' His tone was indulgent.

'. . . is absolutely smashing. It's the one of the mother, Ceres, I think you call her, and her calf playing together in the surf. I've got one adorable sketch of Sausage as he nuzzles his mother under her flipper and——'

'Whoa! Hold on there . . . a study of whom?'

'Sausage,' she repeated.

He looked at her in disbelief. 'You've taken it upon yourself to name the new calves, I gather.'

'I didn't think you'd mind,' she said hesitantly. 'I know you like them all to have names, and you've been so busy you haven't got around to it yourself yet.'

'That's true,' he said, making an obvious effort to remain reasonable. 'I do, however, try to give them names that have some connection, however remote, with science or mythology. But "Sausage"!'

'It's a perfectly suitable name for him!' she persisted staunchly. 'He reminds me of a kind of country sausage we have in Quebec. All shiny and plump—which is, I think you must agree, a very apt description of him!'

She waited, her head cocked, ready to do further battle for her selection. But Adam shrugged. 'I suspect,' he said, 'that this is one argument I'll not win. Sausage it is—but can you see me standing up in front of a bunch of very bright scientists, talking about a whale named Sausage?'

Jensa giggled. 'You'll survive.' In some strange way, she felt in that moment that she had come closer to him.

They headed inland, and the land began to swell into low hills broken by gullies hiding small streams. The greenness increased, in patches at first. It was hardly lush compared to what she had left at home, but after the desolation of the station it appeared positively pastoral to her. They began to pass the odd vehicle on the narrow road. Farm trucks, mostly, and probably on their way to some part of the vast Mendez holdings.

'What's it like around the ranch?' she asked idly.

'Rancho Rosada is built in a valley that holds a fair sized stream. And Felipe has done extensive irrigation —the grounds around the main house are actually very well landscaped. I've always found it pleasant, although Rita gets quite bored, of course, and spends a fair amount of time in Buenos Aires. She has a modern penthouse there overlooking a downtown square.'

'Of course. Rita looked far too lively to be contented down on the old sheep farm for long. Unless, I gather, you're within hailing distance.'

'You can sheathe those claws, if you don't mind,' he said easily. 'I want this evening to go well. If, for some reason, you and Rita didn't exactly hit it off the other day, I want you to keep it to yourself—got it?'

'Got it,' she replied crossly. She was annoyed with herself for having betrayed her feelings about Rita to him. She had no real reason to have taken a dislike to the girl—at least not one she wanted to dwell on. And it was unbecoming to be so catty—it was a weakness she didn't usually allow herself.

In the centre of a broad valley ringed by low hills, they turned off the main highwty on to a private road at the end of which stood tall, wrought-iron gates. Bridging its massive stone columns was an intricate iron arch which spelled out 'Rancho Rosada'. They swung around a curved driveway to the house, an imposing structure of stone and white stucco. It was fringed with gardens lush with semi-tropical trees and plants and, farther out, a maze of smaller buildings.

'Not your average little sheep farm, to be sure,' said Jensa wryly.

Leaving the Rover with one of the many workers that busied themselves around the grounds, they climbed the broad stone staircase, and Adam raised an enormous iron knocker that thudded heavily against the intricately carved door.

Without pause, the door swung open and they were greeted by a white-jacketed butler who bowed respectfully. 'Señor Mendez is waiting for you in the garden room, Dr Ryder,' he said, smiling and indicating the double doors at the end of a long red-tiled hallway.

Adam thanked him, took Jensa's arm, and guided her down the hall. The room into which he took her was part living-room, part greenhouse. The far end was ornately glassed in and contained an exotic collection of orchids. The rest of the room was impressively decorated with old Spanish chests and tables, dark and richly carved. Several low, soft sofas and chairs were upholstered in intense colours.

Jensa's artist's eye took in the numerous paintings by Spanish masters which graced the walls. An ornate chandelier with a span of at least six feet hovered over the vaulted room. The cut stone floor was warmed by the random placement of oriental carpets and native weaving.

The effect was overwhelming—rich, lavish, vibrating. Jensa saw Adam smile broadly and turned to follow his eyes to the far end of the room. The entire wall was dominated by an enormous stone fireplace, tall enough to have walked into. A welcoming fire of whole logs blazed in it. Before it, his hand extended in greeting, stood the wealthy and powerful Felipe Mendez.

'Adam ... how very good to see you again. It's been far too long! I hope your drive wasn't too difficult.'

'Not at all, Felipe. A visit to Rancho Rosada is always worth the trip.' The two men exchanged hearty handshakes, then Felipe Mendez turned sharp black eyes on Jensa.

'Felipe, I'd like you to meet the artist working on my project, Jensa Welles. Jensa, this is Felipe Mendez, Rita's father.'

The older man bent low over Jensa's hand. 'I am delighted to have you in my home, Miss Welles. My daughter tells me you are a very gifted artist. I regret that you have been confined to such an inhospitable part of our country—I hope this visit will provide a pleasant diversion for you!'

'Thank you,' she replied warmly, 'although my stay on the coast hasn't been at all a hardship—I've found a great deal of beauty in the unusual landscape of that part of your country.'

'Ah, but I forget—you have the eye of an artist and no doubt see many details that might escape the less sensitive among us! Come ... sit here by the fire.'

He indicated a deep, down-filled sofa heaped with brilliant velvet cushions. Jensa sank into their depths, revelling in their luxury after the spartan seats of the Rover. She accepted a delicate, gold-rimmed glass of sherry. Adam claimed stiffness in his long legs after the cramped ride and stood by the fireplace, cupping a glass of Scotch in his hand.

'Rita will be down eventually, Adam,' said Felipe, smiling. 'She is engaged in her usual fussing for you!'

'It's always worth the wait,' he replied.

Jensa turned her attention on the man beside her. Felipe Mendez was, she supposed, at least in his fifties, possibly older, but he was remarkably trim. His skin was bronzed, and attractively set off by perfectly groomed white hair and a neatly trimmed moustache. He was not particularly tall, but he had the erect, self-assured carriage that made him a dominating presence in the room.

Obviously a woman-charmer, Jensa concluded, as she sipped at her sherry. He was warm, solicitous, flattering. And very hard not to like immediately. A handsome, wealthy widower like Felipe Mendez would be acutely aware of his appeal to women, and enjoy it.

Jensa felt herself equal to the occasion. She would be pleasant, enjoy her outing thoroughly, and keep him at arm's length, she resolved. Besides, after being tossed between the sneering condescension and crude physical advances of a man like Adam, the polish and charm of a man like Felipe was delicious. When Felipe asked for her permission to call her by her first name, she did not refuse.

The butler was refilling glasses and passing tiny spiced cocktail pastries when they heard the staccato click of high heels on the tiled hallway, and Rita arrived. She dazzled like an exotic bird next to Jensa's paleness. Her long dress was a blaze of magenta contrasting dramatically with the raven curls. Heavy antique jewellery smouldered against her dark skin.

She went immediately to Adam and placed a playful kiss on his cheek, running a scarlet fingernail down the strong jawline. And then, surprisingly, she turned the dazzling smile on Jensa.

'I can't tell you how wonderful it is to have another woman my own age here, Jensa! I have been looking forward to this all day.'

'Thank you, Rita—I have too.' Of course, she thought. Rita will be a model of kindness and generosity in front of Adam. And *I* had to go and get myself chewed out by him for being catty!

'Adam,' Rita said brightly, 'why don't you and I give

Father and Jensa some privacy now to go over her drawings—he has been so eager to see them! You and I can take a walk out to the patio where the men are preparing this evening's food.'

'Of course—go along, you two. You must have a great deal to catch up on.' Felipe beamed at his daughter and Adam.

Adam nodded, smiled briefly, and set his glass on the mantel. Before he left the room, with Rita clinging to one arm, his eyes sought Jensa's, and their message was unmistakable. All right, she thought, watching his back and the slender arm that encircled it. All right ... I'll do my best.

She was totally unprepared by the acute interest which Felipe showed in the drawings. The questions he asked were intelligent and thoughtful. She tried her best to answer his questions, although she felt her knowledge still painfully superficial compared to Adam's.

'Yes ... yes,' he said slowly as he bent over the pages. 'You have a remarkable talent for capturing these creatures, Jensa. I confess that up until now it has been difficult to share Adam's enthusiasm. But now that you have brought them to life, it is another matter ... another matter, indeed.'

Jensa felt a warm flush of gratification. Perhaps she could influence Felipe's decision after all!

Felipe leaned back in the sofa and looked hard at her. 'Let me ask you a serious question, if I may. You are obviously a woman of intelligence and perception. What is your judgment of Adam's ideas? Is there something there truly worth preserving? Or is it just one man's obsession?'

Jensa leaned forward immediately. 'Oh, heavens, no,

Felipe! I've only been there for a short while, but during that time I've read everything I could get my hands on. I have no doubt that everything Adam says is true. If you could only see the things I've seen!' she sighed, shaking her head.

'But I have, my dear—through these drawings. Adam is very lucky to have you. I wonder if he understands that.'

Jensa smiled a tiny, crooked smile. 'That,' she pronounced, 'I'm not so sure of. He tolerates my presence ... barely. He would much rather have the man he hired originally. You heard about that?'

'Rita told me,' he said.

'So far,' she said, and managed a smile, 'we've managed to keep a fragile truce. But I have no doubt that if we were not at the ends of the earth, I'd have been out on my ear long ago!'

'How you underestimate yourself,' he commented, eyeing her curiously. 'Adam is no fool. He knows what he has in you ... the very fact that he sends you to plead his case.'

Jensa's eyes widened.

Felipe smiled gently. 'It's all right. I am well aware of how desperately Adam wishes this land to be set aside as a preserve. And he could not have chosen a more capable—or charming—emissary.'

Jensa felt her heart begin to thud loudly in her chest. She had not realised, until that moment, just how intensely she shared Adam's dream and how much agony she, too, would feel if they were to lose this opportunity. 'Then you are, I take it, considering giving up the land?' she ventured, hearing the slight quaver in her voice.

'Considering, yes,' he replied slowly, running a

thumb and finger down the ends of his moustache. 'But there are problems. I have other, pressing considerations. I confess, my dear, that my decision may have to be made along more practical lines.'

'But the preservation of these creatures *is* a practical matter,' she cried. 'It's not just a sentimental gesture—if more people could only see how fragile the bond is that links them to other creatures ... and how we'll all suffer if that bond is broken!'

'Adam has infected you with his zeal,' he said, smiling. 'But you must not assume that I am insensitive to your point. I understand it ... men cannot tamper with what God has created. But I have many responsibilities, many people dependent on me. I wish I had the wisdom to know what the answer is, but right now, a solution eludes me.'

He became suddenly brisk, and the issue, Jensa knew, was closed. Pressing her hand between his, he said brightly, 'We have prepared a typical Argentinian feast for you, Jensa! We will get your coat and join the others outside.'

'I'd like that,' she said. She'd not push him for any other information on the land, she thought. But she'd give anything to know what the 'pressing considerations' he spoke of were.

At the far side of a broad, flagged patio, Jensa spotted Adam and Rita, huddled together against the cool air, chatting gaily and watching the preparations for the meal. She saw Adam tense slightly when he caught sight of her, his eyes searching hers sharply. She gave a brief, noncommittal smile and turned her attention to the cheerful activities.

In front of them lay a huge pit brimming with glowing charcoal. Over it, on a spit being turned by a grinning, muscular young man, hung a side of beef sputtering in a basting of spicy sauce.

Long tables circled the pit, laden with platters of crusty bread, salads and fruit. A dozen chatting, laughing men lounged near the fire's warmth. 'These are the equivalent of your Canadian cowboys, Jensa,' Felipe explained. They were a colourful sight, dressed in their bright work shirts and leather pants, the various tools of their trade slung from heavy leather belts.

'Do you have cattle, then, as well as sheep?' asked Jensa.

'Oh, yes. We breed very fine beef cattle—some for our own private consumption, but also for the luxury markets abroad.'

'Your activities are varied here—I also saw the oil rigs on our way in.'

'Yes . . . those came only recently, in my time. For my grandfather, there was only the sheep. My father added the coal. And now we have oil. There is a possibility that some day we may be involved in the international market in that as well.'

'To the south?' she asked quietly. 'Where the station is?' She didn't look at him, keeping her eyes fixed on the amber reflections in her glass, but she heard the half-second's hesitation that told her all she needed to know.

They sat under the thickly beamed ceiling of the dining room and sipped coffee and brandy. A delicious dinner had been cleared away by uniformed maids. The air was rich with the aroma of the men's cigars mixed with that of the rare flowers which overflowed from Chinese vases on the carved oak sideboard.

Jensa had watched Adam uneasily throughout the

dinner. He had been gracious, controlled. But a certain tautness about his shoulders revealed a thinly stretched tension in him. She was astonished to realise that she could tell what he was thinking without their exchanging a word.

She watched as he stared, frowning, at the snifter of brandy cupped in his hand. He seemed to make his mind up about something, straightened, and turned intently towards Felipe. Jensa inhaled sharply, afraid for him, and not knowing why.

'I know, Felipe, that this is a social occasion ... but I hope you'll understand if I feel I have to ask you if you've come any closer to a decision about the land. You've seen Jensa's work——'

'Yes, Adam, I have,' Felipe replied smoothly. 'I think you will be gratified to know that I found it very exciting.' He turned his admiring gaze on Jensa.

Rita toyed impatiently with the lace edge on her napkin and looked mildly exasperated that the subject was turning once again to whales. It was a subject, Jensa guessed, that Rita tolerated only because of Adam's fierce interest.

Adam pressed on, politely but resolutely. 'You can agree, then, that what we have down there is a resource of monumental importance?'

'Of course, Adam,' Felipe replied, the slightest trace of condescension in his voice. And Jensa thought at once: no ... no, you do not see. Not really. You consider all this fuss a little amusing and eccentric! She held her breath, feeling the tension crackling in the air.

'I've told you what our organisation is able to pay for the land now, Felipe. But I have high hopes that after this meeting in Buenos Aires, I'll be able to come to you with an amount much closer to the real worth of the land.'

Felipe tapped the long ash of his cigar into a crystal ashtray and extended his lower lip in a pout. 'I think not, Adam. You see, there's oil down there. I've had other offers—serious ones.'

Adam pushed his glass aside and leaned forward in his chair. For a terrifying moment Jensa thought he was going to forget where he was and assume his usual uncompromising manner.

'Yes, Felipe, I know there's oil, and I'm not surprised you've been approached about it. But how does our peninsula enter into it? It's such a small piece of land!'

Felipe's eyes had become veiled, his manner guarded. 'It's not the land—it's the bay, of course. They want to dredge it, make a shipping point for the tankers.'

Adam moved slowly back into his chair.

'You will understand now, Adam,' continued Felipe, almost gently, 'that the issue is no longer so clear. There is money involved ... a great deal. And jobs, Adam, for people who need them badly.'

Adam said nothing. His mind seemed very far away.

They were silent most of the way back to the station. Adam seemed torn between the demands of his own thoughts and the difficult drive over the narrow, unlighted road. Jensa pulled the blanket up around her shoulders and sought a reasonably comfortable depression among the lumps and bumps of the seat.

She tried, without success, to analyse the relationship between Adam and Rita. There was not much doubt that they were on very close, if not intimate, terms. But was theirs a friendship that was headed towards anything? Hardly, she brooded, not when she considered Adam's scathing comments about permanence. And what about Rita—would life with a man destined to live like a nomad, going from one primitive outpost to another, appeal to a hothouse flower like her?

It was laughable, she thought, snuggling deeper under the blanket. But what if Adam were to settle down in some academic position ... become a professor at some big university, maybe in Europe? Rita might like that. No ... no, she thought, blinking rapidly as if to erase some unpleasant picture from her mind's eye.

But another possibility presented itself to her, and she felt her heartbeat increase. Rita was obviously adored by her father, and certainly stood to inherit all of the Mendez wealth—and land. What if she decided to ask for a piece of that land now? Not as a gift for a man with whom she had a passing involvement—but for a future son-in-law!

Stop it, she ordered herself. You're indulging in silly daydreams because you're tired and have had far more brandy than you're accustomed to! I couldn't be jealous of Rita, she argued; there's absolutely nothing about that mindless clothes horse that I envy. Except Adam's attentions? whispered the tiny voice. No! she murmured under her breath, and shifted irritably in her seat.

Adam turned to her, the contours of his face barely outlined by the pale light from the dashboard. 'Uncomfortable?' he asked. 'It's a boring trip, I know. I wish we'd set out earlier. I hate these damned roads in the dark—we'll be lucky if we don't end the night splashing about with the whales.'

'That's a pleasant thought. However, I trust your driving, speedy though it is.'

'Thanks ... I guess.'

'You're welcome.'

'You enjoyed yourself tonight? I noticed Felipe was delighted to have fresh female companionship.'

Jensa made a deliberate effort to overlook the sarcasm. 'Yes. I'd prepared myself for a somewhat offensive masher. But I found him quite charming.'

'Oh, come on,' he snorted. 'I have eyes—you can't tell me he didn't come on pretty strong with you.'

'He prides himself on being a lady's man. No question about that,' retorted Jensa firmly. 'But with him, it's more like some old-fashioned dance ... one with all kinds of elegant, precise steps.'

'And he knows them all, I'm sure,' snapped Adam.

'There's no reason for you to sound so superior, Adam—I seem to recall that you practically ordered me to turn on whatever charm I could muster.'

'And did you?' he asked, shifting the gears a good deal more roughly than was necessary.

'I did my best,' she said coldly. 'But I did it honestly. This project doesn't need any underhand methods to make its value felt.'

For once, Adam seemed temporarily stung into silence. Jensa turned angrily and stared out into the darkness and saw only the reflection of her own troubled face. How fragile the peace was between them! She regretted instantly her sparing with him.

She turned towards him again. 'You're troubled,' she said quietly.

She heard him sigh in exasperation. 'I haven't the first idea of how to fight this thing. If Felipe Mendez is considering selling this land to other oil interests—not drilling himself—then there's money involved here that dwarfs his wealth even. How can I fight that?'

'But the conference at the end of the month in Buenos Aires—perhaps you can persuade people there to throw their weight behind the project!'

She heard his palm hitting the steering wheel with rapid, angry taps. 'Do you have any idea what it's like when people from dozens of countries, representing dozens of different groups, try to make a decision on something like this? Do you have any idea of the red tape we're going to have to hack our way through?' His hand cut through the air with a sharp, angry gesture. 'I got a note in the mail when I went up to Puerto Madryn to pick you up, from another marine biologist working farther up the coast. He's afraid the breeding colony he's studying is breaking up, for reasons he can't begin to figure out. That makes our colony doubly important. We're simply running out of time!'

'Felipe may yet decide in our favour,' she said gently. 'He did say he was still considering it.' But she heard how feeble her words were, given the harsh realities that Felipe had spelled out for them.

They finished the trip in moody silence.

CHAPTER SIX

'SOMETHING is wrong.' Hands on hips, lips pressed in a thin line of disapproval, Maria stared down at Jensa.

Jensa sighed, looked at the few unsatisfactory lines on her sketch pad, and put her pencil down. Smiling ruefully, she said, 'You see far too much, Maria.'

'It is not hard,' pronounced the older woman glumly. 'This is the first time there have been black lines around those pretty eyes. And Dr Ryder—he is like storm clouds this morning.' She tackled vigorously the little piles of gritty dirt that sifted in daily on to the windowsills. 'Things did not go well at the ranch?'

'Things were lovely at the ranch,' replied Jensa, wearily rubbing her temples. 'The house is enchanting, the food delicious. Señor Mendez is a charming host.'

'But,' said Maria firmly, 'things were not all good.'

'Well ... no,' conceded Jensa. 'I'm afraid Adam had some disappointing news about Felipe's plans for the land. And Adam and I ... well, we had our problems.' She slipped off the stool, flicked her cascade of hair off her shoulders, and strode to the window. 'Sometimes, I wish I'd done exactly what he wanted when I arrived —simply taken the next plane out!'

She scanned the horizon until she spotted the bobbing form of the *Lightning* and Adam's black-suited body bent over the equipment. She studied him intently for a moment, then turned her back irritably to the glass.

Maria looked sharply at her. 'Dr Ryder is a smart man about many things ... but about women?' The dark eyes looked towards heaven. 'Sometimes I would like to shake him when I see how he treats you!' She fitted plump hands to the action.

Jensa looked momentarily taken aback, then smiled affectionately at the woman. 'Thanks, but I don't believe for a minute you'd do anything so violent—you're far too fond of Adam!'

Maria looked momentarily chagrined. 'Yes, I am fond of him,' she said grudgingly. 'That's why he makes me so angry!'

'Come on,' Jensa said brightly. 'Put down that cloth! Dusting is a lost cause here. Let's have some of that heavenly spiced chocolate you made this morning, and lament the infuriating ways of our boss.'

'You must tell him when he returns that you are taking the rest of the day to rest,' Maria admonished her, noting Jensa's chilled hand.

Jensa's eyes grew wide with mock horror. 'We took time off yesterday for the trip to the ranch, don't forget—I'm surprised he didn't put me to work when we got home last night!'

Maria remained serious. 'I know how he drives himself, but he cannot expect you to keep up with him!'

Jensa's cheeks dimpled as she watched the alternate pride and annoyance that registered on Maria's face. 'He *is* a demanding employer. And you're a dear to be concerned about me! But I'll survive ... at least for these last days. I confess that anything longer might lay me low.'

Maria remained unconvinced. 'You must see that he treats you properly, or I will have to speak to him! You are different—not like the others.' She broke off, shaking her head.

'Others ...?' queried Jensa, flinching slightly.

'There were a couple. Last year,' Maria replied cryptically. 'Imagine such a trip just for a few hours with him!'

Jensa stared at her, coldness gripping her heart. She wanted to ask who these visitors were, but the words died on her lips. She felt helpless with anxiety. 'Sometimes I think I almost hate him,' she said, her voice almost a whisper.

The older woman hesitated just a second. 'You do not hate him at all,' she said at last. 'I think you feel something entirely different for him.'

Jensa looked up at her innocently. She met Maria's knowing eyes, crinkling at the corners, her face softened by a gentle, worried smile. The expression left no doubt in Jensa's mind exactly what Maria believed that 'something' was.

'Oh,' she said in a whisper that was more like a tiny whimper of pain. 'I ... I don't know, Maria.' But she did. And at once, a peculiar blankness fell over her. She heard nothing more except the thudding of her heart as the meaning of Maria's words rushed in on her.

She was stunned, and utterly bewildered. It had happened, the thing that she had waited for with such supreme assurance. She had at last fallen in love— deeply, passionately, in a way that shook her senses. But with whom ... with what sort of man?

She knew, now, that she had been seized by love for a man who could only mock it. For a man who was not emotionally or morally equipped to understand it, let alone cherish it ... or return it.

Long after Maria had left, she still could not come to grips with it. It was insane, she thought. How could she love such a creature? Perhaps it was all physical, she thought wildly, clutching at any explanation. Yes ... it was just chemistry. A combination of their intense reaction to each other, his admittedly handsome body, their isolation here. She remembered the passion of his embraces and felt her cheeks grow hot.

Then she remembered her profound admiration for his work, the thrill she felt when he spoke of it with such passion and brilliance. She saw his gentleness as the large, rough hand held up the jade-green egg of a tinamou bird for her to see. And she remembered, too, the quiet satisfaction of their long hours spent wordlessly working together.

She knew, now, with not a shred of doubt, that it was not just a physical craving that had shaken her so.

It was a love of the entire man—despite the things about him she could not understand, could not reconcile with all the goodness and intelligence she knew to be in him.

And she knew now, also, with a devastating certainty, that she loved a man who neither liked nor respected her. She shivered, and prayed silently that the time would soon come when she would board a plane and put six thousand miles between herself and him.

Jensa scrambled down the rocky cliff and hoisted herself on to the crude wooden dock. 'Brought your lunch, Adam!' she shouted, hand to her mouth. 'José's engaged in a particularly noisy battle with the car engine and can't come.'

He looked up briefly. 'Thanks.'

She felt herself go weak at the knees, just at the sight of him. 'What are you doing?' she asked, struggling to sound businesslike.

'Checking the scuba gear and underwater camera. I want to get some mother and calf shots before the herd prepares to migrate.'

She lowered herself on to the dock and sat cross-legged before him. 'Looks awkward, all this,' she noted. 'Must be hard getting everything sorted out when you're tossing around out there on the *Lightning*.'

'It's a damn nuisance,' he muttered through a large bite of his sandwich. 'But I can usually depend on José to keep it sorted out.'

'Too bad you won't have him today—I heard him tell Maria he might be with the Rover the rest of the afternoon.'

'Damned bad luck. But I'll have to manage.'

'But it would be so much better if you had an assistant!'

He eyed her sharply across the rim of his cup. 'I detect a gleam of sorts in those violet eyes, Miss Welles.'

'Oh, Adam, *don't* be such a stubborn beast about this,' she pleaded. 'I haven't been the liability you envisaged when you first saw me. Admit it!'

Adam looked intensely irritated, but cornered. 'No,' he admitted shortly. 'You've done much more than I expected.'

Jensa set her jaw at a stubborn little tilt and looked at him unflinchingly.

'I've been swimming and handling tippy old canoes since I was a baby!—please let me go under with you!'

He sighed in resignation. 'O.K. A bully—a nag—that's what I've been saddled with,' he grumbled.

'Then we deserve each other,' said Jensa.

The powerful motor came to life with a deafening roar, and the *Lightning* sped seaward, skimming the surface with rhythmic slaps. In the centre of the bay, it slowed to a crawl, and Adam made wide, sweeping circles, his eyes scanning the surface for clues to underwater activity.

Jensa, zipped into José's wetsuit, thought suddenly that her heart had risen squarely in her throat. Her hands gripped the rope rigging that looped around the boat until her knuckles turned white. For the first time she felt a nibbling of fear and wondered at the wisdom of wangling this jaunt out of Adam.

'I feel very vulnerable all of a sudden,' she said to him with a nervous laugh.

'You are,' he replied dryly. 'Want to turn back?'

She straightened her back and swallowed hard. 'Not on your life!'

'Relax—but be prepared to do exactly as I say, without the usual arguments, should the need arise.' She could not see his eyes behind the dark aviator glasses, but she knew they were fixed on her with deadly seriousness.

'These will bother you when you're under.' He gently brushed back the strands of cornsilk hair that blew across her cheeks and tucked them inside her headpiece. Jensa felt her heart flutter and knew that it was more in response to his unthinking caress than the fact that she would soon face unknown dangers beneath the cold grey waves.

This is *not* the time for foolish fantasies, she lectured herself. Briskly she checked her gear one last time and turned to listen to Adam's stern recital of procedures.

'Well, that's it,' he concluded. 'Last chance for questions, second thoughts, hysterics and such—none allowed when we're under!'

She thought, then shook her head. They'd best get on with it before she lost her nerve altogether. She gave him a quick, brave smile.

He jumped first, swam a few feet, and turned to watch her entry. Giving a silent prayer that she was still half as good as she had told him she was, she positioned her mask and jumped.

The dark waters closed over them, plunging them into a ghostly, silent world of shadows. Jensa felt one terrible moment of panic and turned wildly to find Adam. She felt his hand on her shoulder, twisted, and saw him hovering protectively. The fear vanished.

They had not swum far when she saw his hand rise in warning. He jabbed his hand to their left. Slowly, through the grey mist, Jensa saw two immense shapes emerge, ghostlike, and slide towards them with awesome ease. Adam held her hand tightly.

Let them make all the moves, he had instructed before they dived. She repeated that admonition over and over to herself now, like a chant to ward off danger. She waited agonising seconds as the shapes grew in size and clarity and neared them.

Her tension rose to a screaming pitch as two whales swam steadily in on them, the great eyes swivelling to see what had dropped into their world. They glided to within feet of her and Adam, then turned at the last second with infinite grace and gentleness, and disappeared into the mists. In place of panic, Jensa felt herself flooded with an elation unlike anything she had ever experienced.

Adam nudged her, jabbed upwards with his hand, and they kicked themselves to the surface. Jensa bounced up, pushed back her mask, and only then realised that her lungs were aching for need of oxygen.

Adam shook water from his face. 'A pretty impressive performance, Jensa—I have to admit I was afraid for you when I saw we were going to get the close inspection.'

'Generous praise, I'm sure. And I'll bask in it later on,' she said as they clung to the side of the *Lightning*, gasping for air. The dive had been physically and emotionally exhausting, and her body had been taken over by an odd sensation, halfway between giddiness and a feverish aching. She closed her eyes and rested her face against the arm that clutched the boat. Her breasts rose and fell with laboured breathing.

She heard Adam's breath harsh in his throat and felt the smooth, hard limbs drifting against her own. The current was pushing him against her and threatened to break her grip on the boat. He laid his hand on the small of her back and pressed her towards the boat again, sending a jolt of desire through her.

In the shelter of the *Lightning*, with their bodies drifting weightlessly to the rhythm of the waves, Jensa felt herself overwhelmed by his physical presence. She had been able to fight it before, when she had not understood the nature of her attraction to him. But now, having confronted her love for him, she could not deny her need.

The thin barrier of their suits exposed every line of his muscular body to her softly curved one. She felt her breasts being crushed against his chest, her thighs enclosed by his. He seemed to read her thoughts and sense the longing in her body. In one deft movement he pulled her mask from her head, tossed it into the boat, and bent to cover her mouth with his. Strong lips parted hers, leaving her gasping with the thrill that shot through her.

No! she thought desperately. I can't let it start this time. I never could trust him, and now I can't even trust myself. He would never understand that her desire was firmly rooted in her love of all that was best in him. He would only think that she was another trophy ... that she had played hard to get for longer than most, perhaps, but in the end it was the same.

It was almost impossible to struggle against him in the midst of the rising waves. She thrashed about not unlike some tiny minnow about to be devoured. She looked up and saw the white teeth bared as he laughed at her. 'Oh, come on, now,' he drawled, 'spare me your injured purity routine. If ever I felt a response, it was from you. Let yourself go for once and enjoy it!'

She could not bear the expression on his face. Dear

God, how could I have fallen in love with him? she thought. 'José's signalling you,' she cried desperately, looking towards the dock.

As he turned, she twisted rapidly out of his grasp. Taking a quick breath, she turned bottom to the air, executed a neat dive under the boat and cut quickly towards the shore.

'Jensa—you little fool!' She looked back, being careful not to miss a stroke, and saw him following her. He could overtake her, of course, with the superior strength of his stroke, but her purpose had been accomplished. She could make out Maria watching them from the dock. He would try no more of his seductions with her there!

'For God's sake come back,' he yelled, coming abreast of her. 'It's farther to shore than you think!'

'Not on your life!' she spluttered. 'I'd swim clear to the coast of Africa to get away from your tasteless advances, Dr Ryder!'

A sardonic grin touched his face. 'You wanted those advances—otherwise I would have been the perfect gentleman.'

'Of course,' she snapped. 'Your strongest suit, that!' She didn't know why she was wasting precious breath. He knew precisely how he made her feel—there was no defence against him. How much farther was it to shore?—she was tiring with the tide working against her. She paused and tried to gauge her position.

'Adam,' she said, treading water and pointing towards the shallows, 'could that be another whale over there?'

He scowled into the sun. 'Not so close to shore ... could be a calf, though. Got enough strength left to swim over there?'

'I think so,' she replied, forgetting their argument at once.

Adam and José had managed, with tremendous difficulty, to free the calf from its snare in the rocks. By slow and painful degrees they secured ropes to the battered body, suspended it from the *Lightning*, and towed it to the dock.

Adam had second thoughts about the whole business. 'His mother may have abandoned him for good reason, Jensa. An illness, perhaps, that threatened the entire herd. Or he may be an orphan. We may be delaying the inevitable—he's far too young to survive alone.'

'But can you be sure his parents won't show up?'

'No. But any hope I had that they'd materialise is fading pretty fast.'

'What you're saying, then, is that we should give up without even trying to save him!' she said a good deal more sharply than she had intended.

'I'm saying that maybe it's best to let nature—oh, for heaven's sake, Jensa, stop looking at me like that! I don't want him to die any more than you do!'

He had raised his voice to her, and she looked away quickly, her eyes unnaturally bright.

He shot her an exasperated sideways glance. 'All right,' he sighed, 'all right. We'll try.'

They fought for him for two days. Feeding proved the biggest headache. Jensa mixed condensed milk, corn syrup, flour and vitamins into an unappetising but nutritious brew, while Adam jury-rigged a feeder from lengths of hose and a funnel. 'Not precisely like mother,' he said, 'but it will have to do.'

Jensa had held the funnel over the calf while Adam tackled the frustrating job of getting him to swallow.

At first Muffin, as Jensa had named him, was too weak to swallow. But finally there was a flicker of interest in his eyes and he began to accept their offering. They allowed themselves to hope. He seemed to gain strength, moving from time to time and watching them with intelligent interest.

Jensa decided another type of help was needed.

'Now that get-up doesn't mean what I think it does, I hope,' commented Adam.

'I expect it does, Dr Ryder,' she replied jauntily. She jumped on to the dock, zipped into a wetsuit, mask and flippers joggling gaily in her hand. 'I think a little company might be just the medicine he needs—any arguments?'

Adam shook his head, resigned. 'I'm beginning to know better.'

She flashed him a spirited smile and with a quick twist of her lithe body slipped into the water. She swam gently around Muffin, stroking him and chattering. The calf was delighted and flicked his tail repeatedly in response to her.

Adam sat crosslegged and watched intently as she cavorted with the little whale, sharing her laughter.

'He understands, you know, Adam,' she called out.

'Understands what, my dear?'

'That we're trying to help him. Adam, Muffin doesn't want to die—I *know* that!'

'I have dreadful visions,' he announced, 'of Muffin's mother showing up, indignantly demanding her offspring, and you getting it into your head to dispute custody. After what I've seen today, I wouldn't put such madness past you.'

'Nonsense,' she retorted, splashing a shower of water in his direction.

'Your lips are blue,' he said at last. 'Out with you.'

And Jensa didn't protest when he hauled her easily on to the dock and wrapped a blanket around her shivering shoulders.

It happened, then, with no warning. Muffin's breath became strangely laboured, the too-thin body shuddered. Before they could comprehend what was happening, the little whale rolled slightly to one side and died.

The tears came, but Jensa didn't care. Let Adam berate her for silly, feminine weakness. She had loved Muffin, and she mourned for him.

But there was no cutting remark from him. She felt him enfold her in his arms and rock her gently. He bent and kissed her tear-streaked cheeks, tenderly brushing aside the dampened tendrils of hair. 'We did all we could, you know,' he said softly. 'It just wasn't meant to be.'

She nodded mutely. She understood. But this young creature of another intelligence had touched her so. Nothing would ever be quite the same again.

She waited on the beach.

'Better?' Adam asked, dropping to the sand beside her.

'Not so weepy,' she confirmed with a small smile. 'He's gone, I take it?'

He nodded and draped an arm casually about her shoulders. He had towed the body out of the bay. 'Some good has come out of all this, you know. He taught us a lot. And kept us civil to each other. . . . I never thought I'd run into a girl who'd take to whales and this crazy way of life the way you have.'

What did this sudden tenderness mean? she wondered. Could she possibly hope that he returned even a

little of the affection she felt for him? Perhaps her instincts had served her well after all.

She allowed herself to be pressed to him. This time
she would trust him. A soft moan escaped from her as
his lips slid down her neck to the base of her throat.

'You are so beautiful,' he whispered, and she clung
to him, giving herself over to the sweetness of his embrace.

Breathing raggedly, he held her away from him. 'I
believe this is where you would like me to stop,' he said.
'I hope the effort's appreciated.' His smile was brief and
pained.

'It is,' she replied. 'Some day I may tell you how
much.'

He stood and pulled her to her feet. Hand in hand,
they climbed back up the cliff.

CHAPTER SEVEN

SAND dollars marched around the top of Jensa's work
table in a neat row. She had picked them up on the
beach the day before, entranced by the geometric pre-
cision of the fine etching of lines. Several times she
held them, turned them over in her palm, studied them.

Then, for the hundredth time that morning, she
picked up her pen, made a few desultory scratchings on
her pad, then set it down again, sighing deeply.

'Now what?' Adam's voice growled from across the
room where he sat hunched over piles of charts.

'Nothing,' she said, startled by the sharp tone of his

voice. 'I can't seem to get into it today ... I guess I'm still a little depressed over Muffin.'

'I don't know what the proper mourning period for whale calves is,' he said sharply, 'but I should think you could hang up your widow's weeds now, and get on with it!'

Jensa spun round on her stool to look at him, her eyes enormous. The sleeves of his black turtleneck were pushed up roughly over his elbows and his hair was still uncombed. There was a scowl on his brow.

'I'm sorry,' she said softly. 'I didn't mean to irritate you ... I guess you're a bit out of sorts yet, too.'

'Not especially,' he replied. 'But even if I were, I wouldn't let it stop me from getting my work completed. In case you haven't noticed, we're into our last week now, and there's a small mountain of things to be done!'

'I beg your pardon—but you needn't lecture *me* about the work-load. I was *also* up until all hours of the night,' she replied heatedly. After the calf had died, they had both thrown themselves into their work. It was a form of therapy, she supposed, and in a strange way, a sort of memorial to the little whale who wanted to live but couldn't.

She had worked hard, and she was tired. If Adam Ryder was going to favour her with another example of his temper—well, she could show him a little as well! 'I have no apologies over my feelings about the calf,' she said with dignity. 'And you've not had any complaints about my work!'

'No ... not yet,' he replied unpleasantly. 'But if you keep up this silly mooning, it's a good bet that I'll have a lot to complain about.'

'Is that so—like what, for example!' She slapped

her pen down on the desk and folded her arms across her chest.

'Have you done the series I wanted on the mating?' he challenged.

'No ... no, I haven't,' she admitted. 'But I'll certainly have it done in time—listen to me defending myself!' she exclaimed, bristling. 'You have absolutely no right to speak to me like this!'

'I have every right,' he corrected her harshly. 'I'm your employer, remember? I should have sent you packing the first day. I knew this would happen,' he muttered.

'I don't believe I heard you correctly,' she said in a voice that was dangerously quiet.

He looked at her hard for a second, seeming to debate something in his mind. Then he plunged in. 'I believe you did. But I'll repeat it, anyway. I should have sent you back. You've become a drag on the project with this silly emotionalism. We simply can't afford to indulge you when we're under this sort of deadline pressure.'

'Your arrogance defies belief, Dr Ryder—may I remind you that the reason we're behind schedule on the illustration of the book is that you've asked me to do all this extra display material for the conference on whaling? It's entirely beyond the scope of what I was hired to do, and I think it's pretty low of you to aim any criticism at me. I'm doing double the original assignment—which was pretty heavy to begin with—under absolutely miserable conditions!'

'I don't think I'd have heard Josh whine about the work load,' he sniped.

Jensa felt herself begin to tremble with fury at the injustice of his comments. 'That's a cheap shot—you wouldn't have heard *me* complain about it either if you hadn't attacked me so unfairly and forced me to defend myself!'

From across the room came a loud clattering of pots and pans. It was Maria, reminding them that they were not alone. She gathered up her things, giving Jensa a look that was half sympathy, half warning. As she left them, in stony silence, she favoured Adam a wintry glance.

'There—you see? You and that nasty disposition of yours have gone and upset Maria!'

'I fail to see that *I* have done anything to upset Maria. What is this—a women's conspiracy? I'll complain about the work of my employees any time I see fit—and I see fit right now.'

'I'm glad you told me. You have such a light hand in these matters that I might have missed the message otherwise.' Jensa turned her attention sharply back to her drawing board. Although her hands managed to perform their tasks automatically, her thoughts were far from the lines on the pad. She chided herself for the devastation she was feeling because of his mercurial change in attitude towards her. She had allowed herself to hope, and she had no one to blame but herself.

They worked through the morning in icy silence, the only sounds in the room the scratch of pens, the rustle of paper, the occasional scraping of a stool on the floor. They were each, Jensa was sure, maddeningly aware of the other's presence. If she could judge by the rhythmic tightening of the muscle along Adam's jawline, her presence in the room was as irritating to him as a fingernail on a chalkboard.

How could she have eluded herself into thinking that he was capable of tenderness and respect for a woman?

It was the calf, of course, she thought. It was always an animal that brought out the only speck of decency that existed in Adam Ryder. When it came to her, he had only the same sneering, scathing attitude that she had encountered in Puerto Madryn ... except for those times when his basest needs required her attentions.

And she had *let* him do it to her. That was what hurt so. She had *allowed* him access to her to a degree that she never had before with a man. And it had meant nothing to him. Absolutely nothing.

Oh, she supposed that a man accustomed to the sort of girl who gave all of herself freely wasn't likely to put much value on the much more limited gift she had thought she was offering to him. By his standards, she fumed, what she had offered him was worse than useless. It gave him none of the instant fulfilment he demanded.

She bore down on her pencil and felt the point dig into the paper and snap. Ruined—an entire hour's work on a breaching sketch, good for nothing now but a toss into the already brimming wastebasket.

She saw Adam's exasperated glance shoot her way. With enormous effort she retained her cool demeanour and continued on the now-worthless sketch as if nothing had happened.

Towards noon, she prepared their customary pot of coffee. When she set his mug on his desk, he neither looked up nor spoke. The petty rudeness snapped what little control she had over her nerves. 'Does a simple thank-you not fit into your vocabulary, Doctor?' she flared. 'We women have been liberated for quite a while now—making coffee is a gesture of consideration, not a duty. I realise this may be a novel idea for an antiquated creature like you!'

He looked up at her with studied aloofness. 'I'm not interested in your female hysterics, Jensa. Keep it up, and you'll regret it, I assure you.'

The violet of her eyes deepened. If she had not cared, if she had not seen another side to him, she could have dismissèd him as an uncooth boor. But she did care, and to be treated so shabbily hurt so.

'You know, Adam,' she said, her voice low, 'I feel sorry for you. If you could show a fraction of the consideration to people that you do to animals, you'd be a worthwhile human being. But as it is now, you're contemptible!'

She saw his mouth tighten into a cruel line. 'It should be obvious to you by now, Jensa, that it's of absolutely no importance to me how you, or anyone else, feels about me.'

'Oh, you're your own man, Adam,' she flung out recklessly. 'I've never doubted that. But you've paid quite a price for that independence. You've got sea water in those veins, not blood.'

'Oh? I've always believed I had blood as warm as any man's in me. If memory serves me, I think it's you who turns to ice water, not I.'

'How like you to equate moral standards with frigidity! For you, love means physical pleasure alone, completely divorced from caring and commitment.'

'Commitment, is it?' He laughed shortly, tossing his pen carelessly on to his desk, and lolled back in his chair, one arm draped lazily over its back. As she looked into those mocking eyes, Jensa went cold with fear that he had guessed her secret. She tried to summon the last of her tattered pride. He must never suspect her feelings for him.

'No, not from you, Dr Ryder,' she said clearly. 'Not

even if you were capable of giving it—which you're not.'

'Still denying you feel anything physical for me, are you?' he asked.

She faced him squarely. 'I'm not ashamed to admit that I feel physical passion—why should I? You're hardly the first man who's kissed me. But it has to be rooted to something deeper. You can mock that if you like, but there are many men who don't. It's your loss, not mine.' Her chin trembled warningly, but she stood her ground and her glance did not waver.

He shrugged. 'Schoolgirl nonsense! Life just isn't that way.'

'It is for me. My way of life is just as real, just as valid as yours!'

'I learned very early just how much you can depend on people for constancy,' he drawled. 'I can see you have yet to learn this particular lesson in life. I pity you—I suspect your disillusionment is going to be especially painful.'

He turned his back to her and was immediately engrossed in his work. Emotionally exhausted, Jensa sank on to the sofa and stared at his back. If only you knew, Adam! she thought. I'm having that lesson right now. You're the one who is teaching me how cruel it can be to love.

So much anger and bitterness had spilled out of him towards her. Only he wouldn't call it that, she knew. He'd call it sophistication, experience. Again she felt her insides being torn by that familiar mixture of anger and love that she felt for this man. She just didn't know how much more of this emotional battering she could take from him.

He didn't appear at lunch time, and Jensa ate a solitary meal huddled by the coal stove. It wasn't that Patagonian winters were particularly severe, compared to Quebec winters. But the constant, fine work in the barely heated room caused her delicate fingers to become chilled and achey. The bleakness of the view out the window and the ceaseless whining of the wind did nothing to improve her spirits either.

He'd probably rather starve than eat with me, she thought moodily, eyeing the untouched sandwich she had set out for Adam. She frowned at the pile of notes he had tossed in her direction as he left for the tower. His instructions in the columns were totally illegible.

She had no choice but to bundle up and climb those miserable stairs. Darn him! She debated taking his sandwich with her and decided against it. Let him come and get it himself when he's hungry—it's enough that I fixed it for him after that abominable treatment he gave me!

She toiled to the top of the staircase. With some effort, she managed to wrestle the door shut, closing out the worst of the wind's screaming.

'Sorry to barge into your ivory tower, Professor, but I'm having some difficulty deciphering these scratchings of yours.' She thrust the sheaf of papers at him.

He accepted them silently and began at once to make impatient alterations to the notes. They were scarcely more legible than what he had scribbled before, she noted wearily. She sighed and peered absently into the telescope.

'Can't see a thing,' she announced, swinging it in a broad arc.

'Nor I,' he muttered. 'But that tells us a lot.'

'Such as?'

'The season's changing. I suspect the main herd is preparing to leave for new feeding grounds. The mothers with new calves will stay.'

'Do they migrate far?'

'Thousands of miles, we think. But where they go and how they get there is still a mystery. We just don't know what life is like in the real depths.'

'Do you have any theories about how they find their way to the same places year after year?'

He ran one hand through his still tousled hair. 'Well, they have their own version of a map—they feel the shifts in water temperature. They see how the light filters differently through various kinds of water. They can taste the differences in salt and chemical composition. Then there's the guidance along the ocean floor given by the great oceanic currents, the pull of the moon and sun....'

What an incredible gift he has, she thought. Perhaps he's right. Perhaps it really doesn't matter how he copes with human beings. The knowledge of his genius was awesome to her, yet it left a knot of misery in her throat as well.

'Think of it,' he went on, his face lit up with enthusiasm, 'these incredible creatures gliding through places we may never see, a complete, purposeful society, centuries old.'

Jensa shifted on the stool and his head snapped up at her. It was as if he had forgotten she was there. Instantly, that cold, impenetrable barrier appeared between them.

'Here,' he said, tossing the papers on to her lap. She made a wild grab for them as they began to slide on to the floor.

'I'm going out again,' he said shortly. 'This may be

my last chance. A lot of them may be blown to bits and butchered during the migration. And even if they do manage to make it back, they'll probably find their breeding grounds destroyed by more of what we laughingly call progress.'

He slammed the door and she heard him bounding down the flimsy stairs two at a time. She pressed her forehead against the glass and watched as he disappeared into the shed. Adam emerged a few minutes later dressed in his wetsuit, lugging the scuba tanks after him.

Through the telescope she watched him hoist the tanks on to his back. Then, in his usual unhesitating manner, he jumped over the side of the anchored *Lightning* and vanished under the white-tipped waves. When he at last reappeared, he was not alone. An enormous male had surfaced with him.

Jensa's hands went white around the barrel of the telescope. Adam swam confidently up to the massive, grinning face, stroked it, then slowly eased his way down the length of the great body. Then, in an action that caused Jensa to cry out and tip over the stool behind her, he grabbed hold of a flipper and hoisted himself on to the whale's back.

He'll be killed, she thought in agony. She held her breath until her lungs ached, watching him balance on the broad, slippery back.

But the whale seemed to tolerate Adam with equanimity. He made no move to rid himself of his hitch-hiker. Still, Jensa closed her eyes, weak with relief, when she saw the whale give a slow shake of his head and Adam dive clear of him.

There was no defence against a man like Adam. Just when she had concluded once and for all that he was despicable, he would do something that would sweep away all her misgivings with one dramatic gesture.

He flirts with instant death, she thought. And yet he fears the slightest emotional intimacy. She would never be able to reconcile these two sides of him. She tried to comfort herself that once she was back in the familiar safety of her Montreal apartment she would be freed from this iron grip he had on her emotions. Maybe then she would be able to view him sanely.

Perhaps a civilised man like Ross could give her the perspective she needed so desperately. In his own way, Ross was every bit as skilled and dedicated as Adam. He was a first-rate surgical resident, and she had no doubt he'd make his mark in his profession—without trampling on people's feelings!

But he doesn't excite you, a part of her countered. A decent, refined man like Ross didn't come close to stirring you the way Adam did the first time you saw him. You'd forgive Adam anything—admit it!

'No!' she said aloud. 'I won't go on excusing behaviour from him that I wouldn't take for a second from anyone else!' It was a hopeless argument, one that had raged fruitlessly in her for days now. In disgust, she grabbed the papers and turned to leave. It was then that something caught her eye. A thin trail of dust was spiralling along the road that led to the station from inland.

Rita again? A visit from her was the *last* thing she could cope with today! No ... there was far too much dust being kicked up for her little bullet of a car. Jensa swung the telescope around and brought it into focus on the horizon.

Not one but several vehicles were headed towards them—at least two cars, plus what looked like large pick-up trucks. As they came to the rise overlooking the station, they suddenly veered off and took a disused farm road that led to the far side of the bay. Whoever they were, they seemed to know where they were heading. And their business was evidently not with Adam. Farm people? Not likely—the cars looked far too expensive for that.

Something in the abrupt arrival of unannounced strangers created a distressing uneasiness in her. She had grown so accustomed to their privacy at the station. Even in the short time she had been there, she had come to feel that the bay was somehow their special domain.

She swung the telescope back to the water and saw that Adam, too, had noticed the arrival of visitors. He was standing in the *Lightning*, his legs braced to the rocking of the waves, his hands cupped around his eyes. He was staring across the bay to where the little convoy bumped and bounced to a halt at the water's edge.

Quickly she let herself out of the tower and skipped down the steps. She'd head right for the dock, she decided. If she knew Adam, he'd be heading the *Lightning* for land right now!

'Could you see who they were?' he asked without preliminaries. He yanked the mask roughly from his head.

'No ... I saw just enough to tell me they're not the usual farm vehicles you see around here,' she replied, grabbing the oxygen tank as he shucked it from his back.

His long stride took him quickly up the path to the storage shed, with Jensa skipping to keep up with him. He was inside less than a minute, and came out tugging the old black sweater over his bare chest.

'We'll take the Rover,' he said. They made the short

drive around the bay in tense silence. They both knew that something was wrong—very wrong. Jensa felt her heart constrict with shock as they came to a jerking halt by the trucks and saw the huge jumble of scientific equipment that was already being unloaded.

No one seemed surprised by their arrival. The eyes on them were curious, but not bewildered. She watched with growing apprehension as Adam strode into a knot of men who were directing the activity.

A tall, chunkily built man with black hair separated himself from the group. He smiled broadly and extended a hand. 'You must be the biologist stationed here—Señor Mendez told me we would probably run into you! My name is Faras, here with the permission of my host.'

Adam took the offered hand. The rest of the company remained busily at work, but repeatedly shot covert glances at them. Jensa shifted uneasily in her seat and quickly resolved to join Adam. There was something in the manner of these men that was not entirely welcoming despite the geniality of their leader.

She walked firmly to Adam's side, her eyes straight ahead of her. Adam introduced her as his assistant.

The man made a short, formal bow in her direction. 'Miss Welles is every bit as lovely as Felipe described her,' he said smoothly, and Jensa felt distaste for the self-serving manner.

Adam's voice was sharp with irritation. 'Señor Mendez seems to have filled you in on a great deal, but unfortunately we don't have that advantage——'

'Of course—and I apologise for our taking you by surprise like this. But our business is urgent—time is very costly to us.' The smile, revealing even, white teeth, remained, but it chilled Jensa.

'And what business is that?' asked Adam.

'Oil,' came the reply. 'Perhaps a little out of your field, Doctor, but you will understand nonetheless that each search for a new supply runs into a great deal of money.'

Adam looked around at a large motor launch being hefted out of one of the trucks. Señor Faras noted his glance. 'Of course, this is not the equipment we normally use. This is only to explore the bay's potential as a harbour.'

'This cove could never handle a tanker—in fact, anything of commercial size would do irreparable damage to the ecology of the entire coastline!' protested Adam. 'Surely you must know that.'

'I understand your concern, Dr Ryder—Felipe has told me that some whales breeding around here are a pet interest of yours.'

'Pet——!' Jensa could see that Adam was finding it hard to keep his self-control in the face of the monumental ignorance and conceit of the man. She was terrified that at any moment he would unleash his temper. Nothing would be gained, she knew, by trying to sway someone whose only interest was economic exploitation. There was no room in the minds of such callous, insensitive people for the broader picture.

'I see that we have different perspectives on this issue,' said Adam with iron control. 'I suspect I would be wasting both your time and mine if I tried to convince you that ultimately you'll only be hurting yourself by pursuing this course.'

'You are a perceptive man, Doctor ... but then I expected that. Felipe spoke of you with great admiration.'

'Señor Faras, my permission to run scientific experiments on this peninsula is still in effect for a few more days. I'm afraid I'll have to insist that you explain to me what you intend to do. I cannot allow anything that would upset months of carefully planned study!'

'We intend only a few simple tests—taking bottom samples and so forth. Would this constitute interference?'

Jensa saw the syrupy smile that spoke of nothing but insincerity and again wondered about the extreme self-control that Adam was exercising.

'Not if the tests are carried out cautiously. The main body of the herd is ready to migrate. But there are mothers and newborn calves out there. Your men will have to exercise great care not to run over any of them —they could inflict painful and possibly fatal injuries to the calves with the propellers. And of course,' he added easily, 'your men might even find themselves in an upset which could prove deadly to them as well.'

Jensa felt a hard knot of anger in her chest at the thought that this smirking bunch of interlopers might hurt the calves. Only Adam's tight control kept her from expressing her outrage.

'We will work cautiously, of course,' Señor Faras assured Adam, his voice patronising. He folded his arms across his chest and surveyed the now still waters of the bay in the manner of one very pleased with himself. 'I'm relieved that they're going. That means we'll have no problems with them when we begin the dredging.'

'Have you given any thought to what will happen to the herd when it returns next year and finds its breeding grounds gone—and oil and sewage and beer cans floating among the plankton?' Adam asked scathingly.

'You are a great romantic, Dr Ryder. We anticipated your objections. But the oceans are enormous. The whales will simply move down the coast—this is, after all, only one tiny bay!'

What good did it do to try to argue with such a creature? Jensa raged silently. You couldn't explain to him that soon there would be no other places to move on to. And for these whales, there was no other breeding ground. Their instincts had guided them here through the twilight seas since the beginning of time. And to throw it away so carelessly! She could have wept with anger and frustration.

She looked at Adam, amazed at his calm. Of course, she thought. Adam's far too much the professional to explode at this man. He's trying to size up the situation, determine what his next move should be. She listened with renewed admiration at his casual but purposeful questioning of Señor Faras.

'You heard it all?' They sat in the Rover, at the top of the cliff, looking down at the small scurrying forms of the workers on the beach.

'Everything,' she confirmed miserably.

Adam beat his fist on the steering wheel. 'I thought Felipe understood! I honestly thought that when the time came he would be willing to make a financial sacrifice to save this bay. Lord knows he's got all the money any man could ever need!' He slammed the car into gear and headed back towards the station.

'Does he really stand to make a great deal if this goes through?' asked Jensa, holding tight to the windshield as they rocked and bounced their way down the rutted road.

'Yes, I guess he does,' he replied grimly. 'But I still

say he could make more than enough to satisfy him on just the land alone. My guess is that these guys have told Felipe that they want everything—the land plus easy shipping access—or it's no deal. That business about knowing who we were through Felipe was a lot of nonsense,' he went on. 'They knew damn well who I was and every move I've made down here long before they approached Felipe. They've planned very carefully, giving him a deadline that falls before the conference so that I won't be able to offer him the incentive I'd planned to.'

'What are you talking about?' asked Jensa, turning in her seat to look at him closely.

'I was going to sweeten the financial loss for him by giving him international publicity, naming the trust after him ... you know, giving him some sort of international stature as a conservationist. There are very important people in the world movement—heads of state, royalty, celebrities. I thought Felipe's ego would respond. I was so sure, so sure,' he muttered, shaking his head. 'That's one of the reasons I've been driving you so hard. It was all coming to a head next week— the conference, Felipe's decision. We've even got United Nations involvement and television coverage by satellite.' He slammed his fist on the steering wheel again and brought the Rover to a lurching halt by the house.

'Adam,' said Jensa, 'there's got to be something else you can do. It's not like you to give up!'

'No, it's not,' he agreed, drawing a hand down his face. 'But you tell me—didn't they look pretty smug back there? I have to face it, Jensa, I've been sleeping at the switch on this. Those guys are no amateurs. They've figured out exactly what I'd be able to offer

Felipe and timed their counter-offer to the second.'

She looked at him sharply. He looked depressed, something she would have thought him incapable of. She wished she could give him encouragement. 'What about these people coming to the conference—could you get in touch with them and work something out?'

He looked doubtful. 'They're probably all on their way to Buenos Aires right now, from all parts of the globe. It would be impossible to assemble them in time to present any kind of official position to Felipe. No,' he said, turning to her with a grim expression, 'our only hope is to somehow delay Felipe's decision—convince him it's safe to call the bluff of these oil men by refusing to enter into a contract until we can present another bid. I don't know how I'll manage that . . . beg, I suppose.' He smiled bitterly.

'I'll try with him again, Adam,' she offered.

'I know you would.' He patted her hand lightly. 'But I guess I'm on my own now.' He swung himself out of the Rover and climbed the porch with an unaccustomed sag to his shoulders.

Jensa worked that afternoon with a skill and determination she hadn't known she possessed. She hoped her resolve might be catching, but she could see, now, that she was a complete failure in that regard.

Adam was sprawled on the sofa, his feet propped up on the crate in front of him. The notes on his clipboard which lay on his lap went unread, his coffee grew cold.

Where were his thoughts? she wondered. She knew the answer. They were out there with the great whales, thinking about the journey they were about to start to secret places, wondering if there would be anything for them to come back to when nature urged them to repeat the cycle.

It wasn't only the whales who were in peril here, she thought. It was Adam as well. Whatever she thought of him as a man, she couldn't bear to think of him losing so much as a scientist.

She broke the silence. 'Adam ... what that horrible man said about the whales just moving down the coast to breed. Is that possible?'

He looked up at her slowly. His eyes were tired. He shrugged. 'I don't know ... maybe.'

'Can you *prove* somehow that this bay is unique—that this whole fragile system could be destroyed if these ancient breeding grounds were to disappear?'

He raised one eyebrow reflectively. 'I have no doubts whatever about it ... but from a scientific point of view, it's too early in the research to publish the information I have as fact.'

'Do you have photographs of the same whales coming here year after year?'

'No, but it's something I've been working on. I've been trying to formulate a theory of migration. You might say it's my life's work, really. There was one whale in particular I'd observed last year. I had high hopes ... dreams, I guess they were ... of doing a long-term study on her, maybe even tagging and tracking her.'

Jensa poured herself fresh coffee and Adam held his mug out for warming. She filled it, then curled beside him on the sofa. 'It's funny—but I don't think I remember you mentioning her. Did she come back this year?'

'No, she hasn't shown yet.'

'Tell me a bit about her,' she urged gently.

'She had a very distinct personality. That's why I chose her for the study. Delphi, I called her.'

'Did she have a calf?'

'Oh, yes—a beauty. Tagus was much larger and more vigorous than the other calves. The pair of them were always very easy to spot. Besides her callosities, Delphi had one other feature that made her easy to pick out on underwater film. She had an enormous gash along one side. It was healed, of course. I have no idea what caused it, although I'd give a lot to know. I did some pretty extensive work on them—it's in the files, under Migration Theory, if you're interested.'

'I am—I'll make a point of getting around to looking at it before I go.'

'Speaking of going—I'll not be around tomorrow. I'll be taking the Rover first thing in the morning, before you're up.'

'Is it about the bay, Adam—have you thought of something that might save it?'

'I have some ideas, yes. But I'd rather not say what they are right now. It depends on many factors. And another person, as well.'

Jensa's heart gave a quick thud. Rita? Could he be counting on his relationship with her to sway a devoted father? Her mind raced with the implications of what he had said. Just how far would Adam be willing to go in return for such an enormous favour? She shook her head as if to force away the answer.

She knew she was on dangerous ground. But like someone unable to leave a painful wound alone, she asked him anyway. 'Do you mean Rita, Adam?' She stared into her lap and ran a finger nervously around the rim of her cup.

'I suppose she might be willing to help.' His tone was non-committal.

'She must hold a great deal of sway with Felipe.'

He leaned back and regarded her thoughtfully, his

blue eyes narrowing slightly. 'You're assuming that there would be something in all of this for Rita.'

'I never said that,' she protested.

'But you were thinking it, weren't you? Let me put your mind at rest, Jensa. Rita is quite capable of giving pleasure to someone besides herself.'

Jensa flushed and felt a wave of revulsion sweep over her. 'You needn't feel so smug about people's motivations,' she threw out recklessly.

'What do you mean by that?'

'Only that you think of yourself as being so free, so sophisticated. You're constantly putting people like me down. But all this behaviour that you think of as being so manly ... it's really just that of a little boy crying out for his mother!'

She knew she had gone too far, even before she saw the anger darken his face. She had set a match to the tension that had been rising to the surface in them all day. And now it was going to explode right in her face.

'All right!' he thundered, shooting from his seat and towering over her. 'I've had about enough out of you! I'm no different from any other man who looks for a little pleasure in a world that had damn little to offer! And where am I going to find pleasure, Jensa—from someone like you?'

How could she respond to his taunts? She knew from the depths of her being that she could offer him warmth and pleasure—but not on his terms. And he had made it painfully clear that there was no hope that he'd take them on hers. She turned her head aside and did not answer him.

'No,' he said in disgust. 'I thought not. Women like you are only interested in emotional blackmail.'

She sat frozen in her seat and felt the tears spill down her cheeks.

'What's wrong—afraid I'll try and force myself on you tonight? Well, you needn't be. I'm not interested. I'm a little tired of the lectures you dish out on my subconscious. You're a beautiful woman, Jensa, but it takes more than that to excite a man. I'm going to bed now. I've got a big day tomorrow.'

In one rapid gesture he pulled his sweater over his head. He yanked at the buckle of his belt. It was as if she didn't exist to him.

Her cheeks burning in shame, Jensa walked quietly to the alcove and tugged the curtain closed. She lay across the thin, unwelcoming mattress and felt she wanted to die.

CHAPTER EIGHT

THE scrunch of tyres throwing up gravel jolted her awake the next morning. She jumped from bed and poked her head between the curtains just in time to see the back of the Rover disappear over the crest of the hill.

'Gone already!' came Maria's cheery voice from the kitchen.

Jensa rubbed at her bleary eyes and shook her head. 'You're all a bunch of early birds,' she said, fighting a yawn.

'Breakfast—sit,' instructed Maria, her broad face beaming at Jensa.

Jensa shivered, belted her robe more tightly, and shuffled over to the sofa. 'José has gone with him,' said Maria, setting warm buns and coffee on the crate. 'This morning the generator breaks—he will see if he can get the parts he needs at the ranch.'

'Just what we need at this point, isn't it?' remarked Jensa gloomily. 'As if we didn't have enough things going wrong at the last moment!'

Maria perched on the edge of the sofa and frowned. 'José says things look very bad now for Dr Ryder. It's because of those men who came here yesterday?'

Jensa nodded. 'I think Adam's gone to enlist Rita's aid in swaying her father. Does she have much influence with him, Maria?'

'A great deal, I think. Since her mother died many years ago, she has been the bright light in his life ... the rest is mostly work. And that is why I fear for Dr Ryder—Señor Mendez is a fine man. But he is a businessman. I think, in the end, he will make a decision based on that and not on the heart—no matter how much Rita pleads and sulks!'

What was left then? thought Jensa wearily. The book, of course. She mustn't lose sight of the original purpose of her trip. She looked across the room at the huge pile of drawings on her desk. There was still a tremendous amount of last-minute organising to be done, illustrations to be numbered, captions attached.

She had no patience with loose ends. She wanted to leave Adam with a thoroughly professional piece of work. He was, after all, paying her a very generous salary.

The work would also serve to keep her from imagining what was taking place between Adam and Rita. How unfair it was that she, despite her love for him, was the one who caused all the quarrelling and dissention. It was all so upside down!

She carried her afternoon cup of tea out on to the veranda and inhaled deeply. Adam was right—the season was changing. She tilted her face upwards and felt the sun warm on it. The wind had died, and the air had softened. It was odd then, she thought, that there was so much breaching going on in the bay. Usually they reserved that much activity for stormy weather. She decided to take the rest of her break up in the tower being entertained.

She trained the telescope on a group of whales engaged in some particularly energetic leaping. Something odd about one of them had caught her eye. She twisted the lens into focus and frowned in concentration as the whale leapt and plunged seaward in an explosion of foam. She tensed, looked up at the bay, then bent her head again to the telescope. 'Come on,' she whispered, 'do it just once more ... please!'

She waited an anxious minute, then was rewarded. There was an eruption of spray and the same gigantic shape exploded into view. Jensa shouted with excitement. The long, whitish gash down the side was unmistakable. She'd have to be very sure, though. She jogged across the courtyard and burst into the house with her hair streaming behind her. Maria jumped and a bowl clattered to the floor.

'Sorry if I startled you, Maria!' she cried. She yanked the file cabinet open and flipped through the folders. 'Mating ... Memory ... Migration!' Her hands were shaking as she opened the file and the contents spilled over Adam's desk.

She spread the photos out, chose one, and held it up, sighing in victory. She knew for sure now—Delphi was back. The whale that had played such a major role in years of Adam's research had returned—and not to just any cove along the thousands of miles of South American coastline. But to *this* tiny bay!

It was a miracle. Why wasn't Adam there to share in it? she thought. It was unfair that he be deprived of this experience. She looked down at his notes written in that forceful yet meticulous hand. '... a perfect subject,' he had written, 'intelligent, co-operative. I have no doubt that she trusts me. If she returns next year with her calf, it will be the first hard proof of my migration theory!'

She stared at the exclamation point he had placed boldly at the end of his sentence. She could imagine him putting it there with an almost childlike enthusiasm so unlike his usual hardbitten, cynical attitude. She smiled gently and ran a fingertip over the words, as if in doing so she could touch the hand that had written them.

'Delphi, my dear,' she said suddenly, 'even if your old friend Dr Ryder isn't here, you shan't go without a proper welcoming—I can operate a camera just as well as Adam can!' She tossed the pictures back on his desk, not noticing, in her enthusiasm, that many of them had slid off on to the floor.

She knew she would have to act very fast. There was no telling how long Delphi would stay in the bay. If she decided to move out again to the open sea, there'd be no following her.

Maria was beside herself and pleaded frantically with Jensa on the dock. 'I don't have to understand Spanish, Maria, to know that you don't exactly approve of my little venture!' Jensa tugged at the thick rope that lashed the *Lightning* to the pier.

'Little!' Maria's eyes were enormous with fear. 'I cannot let you do this, Jensa!'

'You're getting yourself all worked up for no reason at all,' she soothed. 'Adam goes out there and plays tag with those whales every day and there's never been an accident.'

'Adam is one thing—you are another!' Maria said sternly.

'And you know yourself that Adam has allowed me to go out with him. Besides, there's hardly a ripple on the water.'

She stepped into the gently rocking *Lightning*, gave one last check to the camera, and looked up at Maria. 'Give me a little shove away from the dock, would you?'

'No! I will not lift a finger in this madness! I will stay here and say prayers for you—even if the whales don't get you, I think there will be no escaping from Dr Ryder!'

'All right. I'll take those prayers—not because of the whales, mind you. But you're probably right about Adam.' Jensa gave Maria a jaunty wave. The older woman responded by looking more severe and wrapping her shawl tighter around her shoulders.

Jensa pushed the boat away from the dock with a paddle. Two strong yanks at the motor cord, and the *Lightning* moved away with a great roar and lathering of foam. Over her shoulder, Jensa saw Maria head for the top of the cliff.

She'd be invaluable, Jensa thought, in keeping Adam from tanning her hide when he found out that she'd taken his precious boat out. But when he found out why she'd done it—that would be another story.

Maria's form grew tiny on the brow of the hill and the plumes of spray from the breaching whales grew larger. Jensa drew her mind away from daydreams about Adam's gratitude and on to the business at hand.

She spotted Delphi quickly and slowed the *Lightning* to a crawl. Then she began the cautious circling pattern as she had so often watched Adam do. Finally, when she had manoeuvred into a good position, she cut the motor.

She got one superb shot after another as the mother and son swam in lazy circles around the boat. Adam had been right—they were a special pair. It was almost as if they were consciously performing for Jensa's benefit.

The *Lightning* rocked unexpectedly and Jensa reached out blindly for the side of the boat. In her excitement, she hadn't noticed that the winds were rising. The surface of the water was already showing white spots where the wind was whipping it into waves. She craned her head upwards and saw that an eerie purple light had filmed the entire arc of sky. To the east, a bolt of lightning tore a jagged gash in the building cloud. There was a storm coming, all right. But it was at least an hour away, she judged. Plenty of time to shoot another reel of film and get safely back to shore.

She crouched on the floor of the *Lightning* and struggled with a stubborn film canister. She didn't notice, then, until she felt the first nudge against the boat, exactly what was happening.

She gasped with shock as she looked up and saw the black arc of the back rise over the side of the boat before slipping into the water. For a moment her heart pounded painfully.

'You scared me, little one!' she cried, releasing her breath in a long, relieved stream.

The calf made several more curious passes at the

Lightning, its human-like eye swivelling, its long flank brushing against the boat like a cat against its master's leg. Laughing delightedly, Jensa leaned out and felt its cool, moist flesh.

'Oh ... you're a fine baby, aren't you,' she cooed, 'all fourteen tons of you. I can see why you were such a favourite of Adam's!'

As she spoke, the water just beyond the calf parted and Delphi's great head appeared. She hung there at the surface, eyes panning the boat, as if curious to see that her baby was all right.

That shot would make one of the most exciting animal studies Jensa had ever seen—she had to capture it. She stood, spreading her legs to brace herself, and framed Delphi and Tagus in the viewfinder.

It happened before she even had time to lower the camera. In one smooth movement powered by her many tons, Delphi arched her back and began a deep, plunging dive. Jensa watched in frozen horror as the flukes rotated and fell towards her.

An edge of the fluke hit broadside, tossing both Jensa and the boat into the air like matches. As her back hit the water with tremendous force, Jensa looked up and watched with a kind of fascinated dread as the *Lightning* flipped and began to come down on her.

The noise of the whales' dive was a deafening roar in her ears, and the pressure of the water pushing in on them excruciating. She felt the sucking force of the water dragging her after Delphi.

As the blackness closed over her, she felt herself being overtaken by a kind of mindless fear. She tried to move her limbs but couldn't. Something was holding her. Something hard was pressing in on her from behind. In front, her face and breasts were crushed against something smooth and slippery. The last of her breath was being painfully squeezed from her lungs.

Her hands groped in front of her. Oh, my God— oh, my God! It's the whale, she thought. Her fingers could feel the smooth flesh. Her lungs ached unbearably now, and still the sucking force pulled her deeper into darkness.

Her last thought before she lost consciousness was that she was pinned hopelessly between the *Lightning* and the whale.

The voices seemed very far off at first. She was still pressed tight against something hard, but her lungs didn't ache any more. She could breathe. I can't be dead, she thought.

Other words drifted through her mind. Careful ... help ... the cliff. Whose voice ... no, voices, she thought. There are more than one. Maria's? Yes ... but why was she crying? And the other voice ... angry, shouting. Her head began to ache fearfully.

She remembered something that sent a shudder through her body. Hesitantly, she reached out with one hand. She had to know what her face was pressed against. If it was the whale's side ... if she was still down there, being sucked after it ...!

Her fingers felt something rough and wet. It couldn't be Delphi; Delphi had felt so smooth under her hands. Her eyes fluttered open, but stung so miserably from salt water that they remained no more than slits.

She could make out Adam's face, though. She could never mistake the curve of that mouth, the line of that jaw. She was in his arms and being carried up the hill.

She had been saved, and she couldn't imagine how.

He bent and laid her on the bed. 'Jensa? . . . Jensa!' The voice was hard and demanding, but she was glad. It cleared her mind and drew her back from that dark place where she had been so close to death.

'Yes, Adam . . . yes. I'm all right.' Her words were a hoarse whisper. She started to ask him what had happened, but her teeth began to chatter in a way that made further speech impossible.

'She'll need those clothes off right away,' she heard him say. 'She wasn't down long, but she could still get pneumonia.'

She tried to raise herself, but Maria was quick, and firm hands pressed her back on to the pillow. 'But I have to explain to Adam,' she protested weakly.

'Yes,' he said, 'you certainly do!'

'Enough!' said Maria, her voice snapping with anger. 'You are soaked to the skin yourself, Dr Ryder. I will attend to Miss Welles—you see to yourself or I will have two sick people on my hands!'

Pain was thudding in Jensa's temples, but if she could only just explain! 'Please, Adam . . . it was Delphi. I thought you'd be happy——!'

'Happy!' he thundered, cutting her off. 'You thought I'd be happy that you pulled a hare-brained stunt like that? You ruin thousands of dollars' worth of equipment and practically give us your own death as the crowning glory to a month of botched-up work— and you thought I'd be happy!'

His face was white with anger. Water dripped from him and formed a pool at his feet. Long strands of wet hair hung wildly about his face. His appearance was terrifying, and Jensa shrank back in horror. She had never, never seen him look like this, although they had come through some very rough times in their short weeks together.

Sick with humiliation, she turned her face away from him and trembled uncontrollably.

'Go—go away from her!' ordered Maria.

Adam's eyes bored into her one last time. Then he spun on his heel and stalked out of the alcove, yanking the curtains shut with such force that they were almost ripped from the rod.

Tears ran in hot streams down Jensa's cheeks. Her spirit had been completely broken. She could no longer hold on to her fragile illusion that Adam felt anything other than contempt for her.

As Maria shushed her and gently tended her chilled and bruised body, she wept quietly but with a pain she had never before experienced. And then, her mind and body strained to the breaking point, she fell into a deep, dreamless sleep.

'Tea time!' A high, trilling voice coaxed her out of sleep.

She willed her eyes open. 'Rita?' she said sleepily.

'That's right, dear! Maria has made you some nice herb tea which she claims will get you back on your feet.' Rita put a tray down on a carton near the bed, presenting Jensa with her dazzling smile.

She was her usual impeccable self, Jensa noted ruefully. She was dressed in a red wool pants suit, gold chains at her neck, the black hair swept up into a cluster of curls on top of her head.

Jensa pushed back the tangle of damp and gritty hair that hung limply about her face. She pulled herself upright, doing her best to straighten the puffy, inelegant flannel nightgown Maria had put her in.

What a sight I must be! she thought. Rita's the last person I want to see me looking like this. No—that wasn't right. It was Adam she wished to avoid above all others. Compared to him, Rita was a blessing.

There was no question that the tea was welcome, anyway. Jensa shoved the pillow between her back and the wall and winced at the darts of pain that shot up her spine and down her arms. Bruises, she thought. Bad ones.

'When did you get here, Rita?' she asked. 'I've been asleep—I don't even know for how long.'

'Not more than an hour,' Rita replied cheerily, pulling a chair up to the side of the bed. She poured Jensa a mug of tea and handed it to her. 'I've been here all along—I came down from the ranch with Adam.'

'Then you were here when ... when the accident happened? I'm still foggy about it ... and somehow I'm not sure I want to hear what I can't remember.'

'Small wonder!' cried Rita, raising her eyebrows theatrically. 'I saw it all very clearly from the top of the cliff. Maria was there—she told us what you were trying to do.'

'I remember the whale diving,' Jensa said quietly. 'And I remember being crushed ... or pinned, somehow. And then nothing ... until I woke up in Adam's arms.' She raised her eyes and looked into Rita's imploringly. 'Tell me exactly what happened, Rita—I'm afraid to ask Adam.'

'I don't blame you at all, Jensa,' she said. Her voice was soft with sympathy. 'I told Adam he was being a monster, but you know how he is!' She rolled her eyes dramatically. 'I have never seen him so furious as he was when we saw you out there in the boat. He demanded that Maria tell him what was going on. Poor

Maria—she was trembling so she could hardly choke the words out!'

'I hope he's not blaming her for any of this,' said Jensa miserably. 'She tried to stop me, but I was just so sure that I could do it!'

Rita shrugged. 'Well, no matter,' she replied, dismissing Jensa's concern for Maria. 'His anger at her was soon forgotten. The next thing we knew, he was tearing down the cliff like a madman, shouting something about the boat and the cameras and the waves—I guess he was afraid you would lose them or something. He yelled for José to come with him.'

Jensa pressed her eyes shut and shook her head as she imagined the commotion that had been going on behind her as she so blithely snapped pictures.

'I am upsetting you—perhaps I should stop!' cried Rita, patting Jensa's hand.

'No! Please—I need to know.'

Rita took a deep breath and launched into the remainder of her narrative. 'Well—off they went in the other boat and they had just come up behind you when —poof!' Her hands made a dramatic, exploding gesture, and Jensa flinched as she remembered the crash of the whale's body against the side of the *Lightning*.

'Both you and the whale disappeared. And the boat, too!' said Rita, the beautiful eyes growing bigger. 'Maria and I just hung on to each other and prayed because to us—it was the end!'

'My feelings, too, about that time,' remarked Jensa wryly. She took another sip of the herb tea.

Rita rushed on, obviously enjoying her dramatic tale. 'But Adam, he was into the water, too, quick as lightning. He vanished after you. Maria wailed, and I kept on praying. But the next thing we know, up comes Adam ... and in his arms, he has you! José fished you both out. And the rest ....'

'The rest,' sighed Jensa, 'I know only too well.'

'But you were only thinking of the research. Certainly you never meant to scare us all to death and lose those things!'

'Things?' said Jensa weakly. She sighed and collapsed deeper into the pillow. 'Of course. The camera ... and the recorder. And the *Lightning*?'

'Smashed,' Rita said flatly.

Jensa groaned. 'When I decide to mess something up, I certainly do it in a grand manner, don't I?' she said miserably.

Rita became suddenly very serious. 'Jensa ... that brings me to the real reason for our little talk. I hope I can make this as painless as possible for you.'

'I suppose you're referring to what's ahead between Adam and me.'

'Yes ... he wishes, of course, that he had followed his first instincts and not let you come here.'

'I see,' said Jensa quietly. 'Well, what can I say? He's perfectly right. I've mucked things up and almost killed him in the bargain. I suppose,' she said, 'he'd like me to go right away.'

'That's what he's asked me to tell you. I think you can see that it's the only way ... for both your sakes.'

'I'm more tired than I realised,' replied Jensa softly. 'I don't think I can face Adam. Not right now, anyway.'

'I understand. Would you like me to tell him that you'll go?'

'Would you mind very much?'

'Of course not. Oh—and one other thing. Adam said

to tell you that José will be free to drive you into Puerto Madryn first thing in the morning.'

'Fine,' Jensa agreed dully. 'And Rita—would you also tell Adam that I'll reimburse him in full for all the damage? It may take me a while, but if he'll just notify me in Montreal as soon as he has it all figured out ....'

'I'll tell him. You sleep now, Jensa. I'll have Maria take care of your packing. By tomorrow afternoon you'll be in Buenos Aires and you can start putting all this unpleasantness behind you.'

Jensa nodded mutely and burrowed deeper into the covers to hide the tears that were once again flooding down her cheeks. Rita tiptoed out of the alcove, pulling the curtain shut.

The house was silent when Jensa woke the next morning. Her suitcase sat packed and waiting just outside the alcove. The sight of it made her bite her lip. In anguish, she turned back to the mirror and continued brushing the sand from her hair. She could manage nothing but a dull and untidy bun at the back of her neck. It would have to do, she thought wearily. She tossed the last of her things into her make-up bag and clicked it shut.

She was pouring herself some coffee when the front door opened. Adam entered the room, and there was a moment of crackling tension as their eyes met.

Jensa lowered her long lashes. 'Good morning,' she said quietly.

He returned her greeting without expression, then added, 'You're ready to go?'

She nodded and indicated her bags. 'Whenever it's convenient.'

'There's a regular flight out of Puerto Madryn for Buenos Aires mid-afternoon,' he said stiffly. 'You'll have no trouble making it.'

Feeling horribly self-conscious, she put down her coffee and went over to the desk. 'I was up a bit during the night . . . I guess you were on the beach. I sorted the drawings, got them in some kind of order. The things for the conference are in this pile.' Her voice petered out. There was such reproach in his eyes she could hardly bear it.

'José's outside . . . I guess it's time to go,' he said.

'I should have done it long before this,' she said.

'You'll be relieved, then.'

'Yes . . . I suppose we both will be.'

She watched him go out of the house. He hadn't even said goodbye.

CHAPTER NINE

FROM her hotel window Jensa could see the broad, tree-lined boulevards of Buenos Aires sweeping down to the harbour, while the narrow streets of the old town snaked out on every side, alive with noise and colour and movement. It was different, indeed, from the endless expanse of treeless grey desert that had encircled the research station.

Jensa toyed with the edge of the curtain, and debated. At first, she had just wanted to grab the first available flight and skulk away in defeat. But it would have been a humiliating departure. And she still hadn't decided how to break the news to Josh. He hadn't hesitated a second in recommending her as his replacement —what on earth was she going to say to him!

She slipped down from the window ledge and began to pace the room restlessly. She mustn't give in to this building self-doubt, she warned herself. If she did, it was going to be a disaster, both personally and professionally.

Besides, she thought, feeling the beginnings of a small rebellion, she wasn't the only one who was at fault here! Adam would have to take some of the blame for this fiasco—he'd given her no chance from the beginning!

Outside, Buenos Aires was beginning to warm and shine under a bright sun. How often does a working girl get to be in a famous South American capital? she asked herself. She'd be a fool not to spend these last few days there, before returning to be assaulted by the building Canadian winter.

Her resolve strengthened. She picked up her handbag from the dresser and removed an envelope from it. José had given it to her just before she boarded the shuttle flight in Puerto Madryn. It was her pay cheque, of course; she had known without asking. How humiliating it was that Adam hadn't been able to give it to her himself, but had left it instead for poor José to do.

She slipped the cheque from the envelope and studied it. It was for the same generous amount Adam had originally offered to Josh. He had not reduced it for her early departure. There was no mention of what she owed him for the lost equipment. How much did he resent having to pay her? she wondered miserably.

Stop it, Jensa! she lectured herself. One mistake didn't destroy the dozens of beautiful drawings and charts she had prepared! She had more than earned her salary.

She studied the bold handwriting and saw her own name written by him for the first time. Her heart lurched painfully. Holding that slip of paper was like still having a tiny piece of him with her. She saw that the cheque was drawn on a Buenos Aires bank ... there'd be no trouble there.

At the hotel bank, she converted it into traveller's cheques. She set aside a prudent amount for contingencies and resolved to spend as much of the remainder as she wanted in some sort of extravagant consolation.

A growing crowd milled about and she found it difficult to thread her way through the lobby. Bus arrivals from the airport, she thought, as she excused herself and squeezed through knots of people and piles of luggage. She heard a half a dozen languages being spoken by festive groups of people who waved and chattered and embraced.

She ducked around a marble column and almost tripped over an easel set before the entrance to one of the ballrooms. She read the sign tacked on it and felt a jolt of understanding. Of course—how could she not have connected it! It was the international whaling conference. That accounted for the mosaic of costumes and faces, the abundance of people with press badges, the film crews lugging their heavy equipment and snaking lines of cable.

She scanned the programme list on the poster. There was a variety of seminars from which to choose, an address from a representative of the United Nations. And, listed in bold letters, the keynote speech to be given at the opening banquet—by Dr Adam Ryder of the United States. His subject—The Southern Right

Whale: Breeding and migration patterns, and the need for aggressive preservation measures.

Panic rose clear and hot in Jensa. She turned on her heel and scanned the lobby, sure that Adam would appear in front of her as if by magic and tear at fresh wounds in front of all these people. How could she be so stupid! she thought. She'd chosen this hotel because of its fine reputation—she should have realised that it would be selected for the conference for the same reason.

Adam was nowhere in sight, of course. She realised her panic had been silly; he would still be at the research station. She slipped out on to the boulevard and was swallowed up in the morning crowds.

The sun was already strong, and she slipped large sunglasses over the fine bridge of her nose. Lifting her chin to a confident angle, she walked briskly past the gay shop windows. She'd have to keep a sharp eye out for Adam, of course, she told herself. She didn't want any awkward meetings with him—no doubt she would also be faced by a decorative, and possessive, Rita Mendez clinging to the arm of the conference's biggest celebrity. She imagined such a scene, shook her head, and increased her pace.

No, she would not slink about the hotel like an outcast. She was on neutral territory now. Adam could no longer act the petty dictator. The more she thought about her humiliating departure the angrier she got. Not one word of thanks from him! She stared into the window of a luxury boutique but saw nothing but Adam's face, mocking and derisive.

She bristled with packages and barely made it through the lobby door.

'You have enjoyed your shopping, Miss Welles?'

said a grinning bellhop as he rushed to relieve her of a precarious pile of boxes.

'Indeed I have,' she said, returning his smile. 'Your shops are absolutely gorgeous!'

The boy looked pleased and pushed the elevator button with an elbow. In fact, Jensa was a little startled by her extravagance. She didn't usually surrender to such self-indulgent whims. But today, it felt good.

Some of it was for friends and family, of course. Argentina had some of the finest leather goods in the world. She had bought exquisite purses for her mother and Evie, and a native poncho for her father. She'd not forgotten Josh, either. As an artist, he would appreciate the charming native wall hanging she had picked up in a craft shop. And the vibrant local textiles she had selected for herself would brighten her apartment over the long dark days of the northern winter that stretched ahead of her.

She was suddenly weary. She'd bathe, change, go down for a sensible, early supper, and then right to bed, she decided.

In spite of her resolve to stay well out of the way of the preparations for the conference, she found herself drawn irresistibly to the broad doors of the ballroom which now stood flung open. Only a few people were inside—organisers, busy at work at tables near the front.

Large display boards were ranged down one side of the room. She blinked—could it be? She took a few hesitant steps inside the door. Yes ... she knew all of it like the back of her hand. It was hers. Dozens of her drawings and charts were there, all neatly mounted and labelled.

She bent, read, and recognised at once Adam's large, rounded printing. He must have been up all night preparing all this, she thought. She could picture him sitting at her desk, fussing and growing angrier by the minute, biting down on the stem of his pipe as she had seen him do so often when his temper was rising.

She walked slowly from board to board, feeling herself caught up again in the excitement of their work. We should have shared this moment together, she thought—and we would have, if you hadn't been such an impulsive little ninny!

He had warned her, after all, many times. But she had acted as if she knew everything. She *had* been a fool, just as Adam had said. Jensa Welles usually found profanity as boring as it was unpleasant, but now she permitted herself a mild oath and thought she might be forgiven. Standing there, looking at her own work as if she were a complete outsider, she realised fully just how much her stunt had cost her.

'They're quite something, eh?' The voice was quiet and heavily accented. Jensa turned and looked up into the eyes of a tall, rangy man. The strong-boned body was comfortably clothed in well-worn tweeds. A shock of white-blond hair fell across a friendly face.

'Oh ... the drawings, you mean?' she replied, summoning a quick smile.

'Yes—I noticed you were quite lost in them. They're excellent, don't you think?'

'They're fine,' she replied casually.

The stranger inclined his long body and studied a picture of breaching. 'Adam was really very lucky to find an illustrator who could capture something like that—it was a woman, you know,' he added.

'Adam ... you know the man who is responsible for this project, then?' she asked, keeping her voice as conversational as possible.

'Oh, yes. Adam Ryder and I have been friends and colleagues for a long time now. We worked together on an ocean-going research vessel in the North Sea several years ago. Of course, our work now keeps us separated by half the globe, but we still correspond regularly about our whales.'

The man grinned and pointed to the name tag on his lapel. 'My name's Sven Hamsen—from the Norwegian delegation, by the way. Are you here for the conference too?' His eyes travelled to her collar, bare of any name tag.

'No,' she said quickly. 'I'm just staying at the hotel for a couple of days ... sightseeing,' she added weakly.

He looked slightly disappointed. 'You seemed so interested, I thought you must be a professional of some kind.'

Jensa wondered if she had offended him by not offering him her name. She smoothed over the momentary awkwardness by asking him a question about one of the charts.

Mr Hamsen brightened immediately. 'We are always eager for converts to our cause,' he said. 'If you would like, I could tell you a little about what we are making such a fuss about here.'

'I would like that very much,' she replied warmly. It was impossible not to like this hearty, open man. They strolled from board to board, chatting, pointing, questioning. The man was obviously delighted by Jensa's intelligent interest in his favourite subject. He confided to her that his own special field was the elusive and beautiful narwhal, prized for its six-foot-long unicorn's horn.

A *friend* of Adam's, thought Jensa as she listened to him. There had been so many times when she would have said that no such person could exist. Yet here he was—he spoke of Adam with such evident affection and respect. He too must know the other side of the gruff, abrasive man she had first encountered. At least she hadn't deluded herself entirely.

They came to the end of the display and the man pointed to a large card. Illustrations by Jensa M. Welles, it said, followed by her business address. Well, at least he had given her due credit, she thought.

'Just a young woman, according to Adam—but such beautiful work! I asked him if he intended to use her on his next book.'

Jensa said, perhaps too quickly, 'And what did he say?'

'No,' he replied, looking puzzled. 'He said it hadn't worked out. I thought it strange . . . and a great shame, don't you agree?'

'I guess they had their reasons,' she replied tensely. She didn't want to be rude to this man, but she knew she had to get out of there. She thanked him and walked quickly out of the ballroom, keeping her head down and avoiding the milling groups of people beginning to gather around her work.

She ate her supper slowly and lingered over tea until she was sure the conference delegates would all be safely at the opening banquet.

As she passed the half-open door of the ballroom she could see that dinner plates were being cleared. The lights had dimmed throughout the room, falling only on the head table.

The sane thing to do, of course, was to walk firmly in the direction of the elevators. But doing the sane thing had not been her habit of late. She peeped around the door jamb and saw that it was very dark at the back of the room. There was no way she would be seen.

A smiling waiter approached her questioningly. From his gestures, she understood that he was offering to show her to a seat.

She whispered her thanks in his ear and pointed to indicate that she wanted just to stand there at the back. The waiter grinned and nodded shyly. Obviously, anything the beautiful blonde foreigner wanted would have been fine with him. Flustered, he tiptoed back to his station.

Jensa's eyes moved along the head table. She saw him, and was electrified. He was leaning back in his chair, turned somewhat to face the speaker. His head was tilted to one side in concentration. She knew that mannerism of his and loved it.

He was dressed as he had been for the dinner at the Rancho Rosada, in the same impeccable beige suit and plain white shirt. The long, slender fingers held the battered pipe. A cup of coffee sat in front of him. She was as stunned now as she had been that day at the transition in him from crudeness to refinement. It sent tiny prickles of excitement down her neck.

Rita. Was she there, too? Her glance went rapidly from face to face at the head table. Just officials, apparently. But in the audience? It was too dim to tell. But if she was there, she must be feeling the same thrill.

At last it was Adam's turn to speak, and the room buzzed with excitement as he rose to warm applause.

These experts obviously didn't anticipate just another dry after-dinner speech. Every eye was riveted on him. Jensa felt her palms go damp and her heart thud painfully as he pulled the microphone towards him.

He was impassioned. He was spellbinding. He spoke with vision and urgency, sparked by sharp humour and an infectious delight in his subject. His strong, clear voice rose and fell, paused, then rushed forward, while the expressive hands cut through the air to underline a point. Jensa's eyes shone and she hugged herself as she drank in every word.

Then she heard him speak her name. '. . . so many of you have commented on Miss Welles's remarkable illustrations. You will be happy to know that many more of her drawings, capturing things never before illustrated, will be in my latest book on the right whale. I am most grateful to Miss Welles for the gift which she brought to our work, for her untiring dedication under what were, at best, the primitive conditions at the research station.'

Jensa felt the sudden sting as her eyes filled. She bit her lip to keep the tears from spilling over. 'And now,' she heard him say, over the beating of her heart, 'I would like to make an announcement . . . one that I hope will set a tone of optimism for this conference.'

It was what they had worked and prayed for. The land around the bay had been acquired for a sanctuary. The bay would be safe for the whales! And in addition to the peninsula, another large strip of land had been purchased and donated to the sanctuary anonymously. It would act as a buffer zone to protect the bay from any future industrial development.

It was a stunning victory. There were excited exclamations and thunderous applause from the audience.

Jensa did not try to hold back the tears now. She let them flow freely as she listened to a relaxed and jubilant Adam explain the details of the Mendez Wildlife Sanctuary and Research Centre, as it was to be called.

The lights rose, an eager crowd surged forward to congratulate Adam, and Jensa slipped unnoticed from the room. The glass-fronted elevator swept her silently up over the glittering lobby now filling with the crowds spilling out of the ballroom. Rita, she thought, must be responsible. It had to be. She must have intervened with her adoring father on Adam's behalf.

In stockinged feet and skimpy lace slip, she stood before the bed and shook her shining blonde head. She still could not believe that she had allowed such a self-indulgent urge get the better of her more sensible, thrifty nature. She sighed in mock despair. 'Well, Jensa, what's done can't be undone. And surely waste is as great a sin as extravagance!'

She reached into the jumble of shiny boxes and snowy tissue paper that smothered the bed and extracted a silk blouse the colour of fresh country cream. She slipped the deliciously cool fabric over her bare arms and looped the long ties in a floppy bow at her throat.

And then the suit. She had never before owned anything quite so luxurious, she thought, as she felt its buttery soft suede slide over her smooth young skin. It was a perfectly simple mid-calf style done in a subtle wheat shade. She brushed the stream of cornsilk hair and let it fall simply over her shoulders.

She had made a resolution that morning, as soon as the intense South American sun had streamed into her bedroom, that she wouldn't waste her last day in

Buenos Aires. She was booked on a night flight to New York. Most of her bags sat packed and waiting for the bellhop. She intended to spend the entire day visiting art galleries.

Her eyes fell on a tall, slim box. She opened it, pushed the tissue aside, and pulled out a supple pair of high suede boots with slender heels.

'Jensa Welles,' she said sternly, 'if you even consider wearing new boots on a gallery walking tour, you'll deserve every single bump and blister!' She smiled, remembering how striking they had looked with the suit, and shrugged. 'Blisters it is,' she announced.

She extended a length of slender leg and pulled on one boot. There was a sharp rap on the door. The bellhop, she thought, calling: 'Just a second!' She grabbed for the other boot. She stood, pressed her skirt down, and crossed the soft, thick carpet to the door.

'My bags are——' Shock and pleasure and fear and doubt all crowded in on her in rapid succession. 'Adam!' she said softly.

'Hello, Jensa. May I come in?'

She hesitated much too long, but he made no move either to go or enter. 'Of course,' she said at length. 'I'm sorry.' She stood back to let him pass, struggling to control the trembling that had started in her hands. 'I didn't expect to see you,' she said coolly. 'How did you know I was here?'

'A friend told me,' he replied with equal coolness. 'Sven Hamsen.'

She looked startled. 'Mr Hamsen? But he didn't even——'

'Know your name? No, he didn't. But you made quite an impression on him nonetheless. He went on at some length about the beautiful Nordic-looking girl he'd met at the display. He couldn't stop marvelling that anyone who looked like that could be so intelligent. Quite won him over, you did, with all those questions about the subject closest to his heart.'

'I see,' said Jensa, nettled by that familiar, patronising tone of voice. 'And you decided I must be the girl?'

'There isn't exactly an over-supply of leggy blondes conversant on the life cycle of the right whale, you know.' He stood eyeing her teasingly, one hand thrust into the pocket of his beige slacks. Unwilling, she took in the good tweed jacket, the cashmere turtleneck. Her stomach gave the little flip it always did when she was close to him.

She dragged her eyes off him. 'You needn't be so patronising!' she snapped. 'I'm sure there are many women at the convention who are quite capable of holding their own in an intelligent conversation.'

'You're quite right, of course,' he acknowledged. 'But then you usually are, aren't you?' He sat without invitation on the sofa and raised an ironic eyebrow. Jensa refused to be drawn into verbal games with him.

'I suppose you've come about what I owe you for the things I destroyed. Have you been able to come up with a figure yet?'

He looked puzzled for a second, then said, 'Oh, that. I was going to write to you. You needn't worry—the *Lightning* was found aground on the other side of the bay. Damaged, but insurance will handle it.'

Jensa breathed a sigh of relief. 'And the camera?'

'Fished out safe and sound. One of the reasons those things are so devilishly expensive is that they're built like small submarines—watertight, shock-proof ... with floats and markers, of course.'

Jensa allowed herself a small smile. Then she had a

thought. 'And the film?' she asked abruptly.

'Snug as well. And the clincher to my last year of research, I might add. The shots are excellent—also dramatic, given what happened after the last picture on the roll ... you know, the one where Delphi raised her head to see what you were doing with her precious baby?'

'You know, Adam,' Jensa said with sudden seriousness, 'I've regretted leaving in such a huff that I didn't get to say certain things. It must have seemed to you that I took the incident lightly. I didn't, of course. I haven't slept properly since it happened. I'm painfully aware,' she went on, her eyes downcast, 'that I almost got both of us killed. I'm ashamed that in all the uproar I never even thanked you for saving my life.'

'I won't say any time, Miss Welles ... but you're welcome, nonetheless,' Adam replied dryly. He looked at her bags stacked by the door, then ran his eyes over her in that frankly appreciative way that never failed to bring colour to her cheeks. 'I take it you're on your way out—am I keeping you?'

'Not really. I have a late flight home tonight. I was just about to go gallery-hopping.'

'Commendable. But they can wait a little, can't they?' He pulled back the sleeve of his jacket with a well-manicured finger and glanced at a gold watch. 'I have a seminar myself shortly. But there's something I want to tell you about. Why don't I call room service and order us up some coffee?'

She nodded her approval of the coffee and listened as he dialled and ordered for them in fluent Spanish. By the time he returned to the sofa, she was unable to contain her enthusiasm. 'It's the Mendez Sanctuary, isn't it?'

He leaned back and took a long look at her. 'I thought to surprise you,' he said.

She was momentarily flustered but recovered herself. 'I'm sorry,' she said, 'but I did hear. Your group has pretty well taken over the hotel, you know. There's been a lot of buzzing about it on the elevators and such.' That much was true, she thought, and would have to do. She had no intention of revealing to him that she had crept into the ballroom, charming the waiter shamelessly so that she could hear his speech.

'I'm terrifically pleased,' he said. 'We came very close to disaster there.'

'I'm very happy for you, Adam. Rita must have been very persuasive with Felipe. I'm sure you're grateful to her.' She spoke quietly but with sincerity.

'Rita? She had nothing to do with it—whatever gave you that impression?'

'You did, of course. Don't you remember? You said that the outcome depended on another person, and I assumed. . . .'

'Rita, of course.' He smiled. 'The way you harp on about that young lady makes me think that you're not exactly indifferent to me. My dear girl, did you really think that a million-dollar land deal would stand or fall on the batting of some beautiful black eyes, even if they did belong to Felipe's darling daughter?'

'Well, not if you put it that way,' she replied. 'I'm not that naïve. But I thought that Felipe might have other . . . considerations . . . in connection with the land and Rita, and you. . . .' Her voice petered out lamely.

'Jensa, I do believe you're starting to babble,' Adam said severely. 'What other considerations?'

She threw up her hands in defeat and sank back on

the sofa. 'None,' she said flatly. 'Let's skip it. I guess I'm all wet on this.'

'An apt description,' he drawled.

'If I'm wrong, then, who *was* the other person you were referring to?'

'My mother,' was the reply.

'Your mother?' she cried.

Curled on the sofa, a cup of coffee in her lap, she listened intently as Adam paced before the tall windows and told the complex story of the last-minute negotiations for the land. He talked of escalating bids, bluffs, telephone calls and cables from around the world, all-night bargaining that had started tough and become steadily tougher.

'We never expected Felipe to give us the land out of the goodness of his heart—not after the oil was discovered, that is. But I give him full credit. He bent over backwards to give us the best possible shot at it. In the end, he took a considerable loss on the deal—our highest bid was substantially under what the oil company was offering. I don't mean to make him sound like a saint—by most people's standards, he still did very well. And then, of course, he's getting his little bit of immortality by having the preserve named after him. He'll get generous media coverage around the world ... we'll see to it.'

'And the men on the beach?' she asked, fascinated.

'Oh, they've done all right, too. They're buying from him farther inland—grumbling, no doubt, but they'll manage.'

'But how on earth did you raise so much money?'

'For the peninsula itself, matching funds—half from the government, half from our international organisation. The larger buffer zone was a gift from my mother.'

Jensa stared at him in utter disbelief. 'I can't believe my ears, Adam—after what you said about her?'

He came and sat beside her. 'It was what *you* said about her that made me call her in New York.' He saw the confusion in her eyes and said, 'I mentioned, I think, that my mother is loaded—through birth, divorce, remarriage. This isn't the first time she's offered me such a generous sum. She had always known, I guess, better than to offer it to me directly. But she had approached me about a trust fund for any research I wanted to do.'

'And I can imagine,' said Jensa gently, 'what your reaction to that was ... you assumed it was an attempt on her part to buy forgiveness.'

He nodded. 'Right—I always turned her down cold. And with a vengeance.'

'Then what made this time different—the urgency of the situation?'

'Surprisingly, no. That day we talked—up at the sea-lion colony—you got me thinking about how *I* was being cruel ... perpetuating an old wrong. My abandoning her in her old age was no more excusable than what she had done to me as a child. At any rate, I called her, told her I needed her help. She was delighted, gave us the go-ahead to establish the Edmund Ryder Marine Research Foundation—after my father. Pretty impressive, eh? Its first major grant was for the land.'

Jensa looked at him for a long while without speaking. Then, 'It's changed you,' she said, 'hasn't it—this coming to terms with your mother?'

'Good lord, no!' he protested, laughing. 'We don't fool ourselves that we're now magically and lovingly reconciled. But at least we're much more at peace with each other. I hate to disappoint you, but I'm the same tyrant I always was.'

Jensa could see that he was not—at least, not entirely. She steered the conversation back to less sensitive matters.

'I haven't seen Rita or Felipe around the hotel—but I expect they'll be here to celebrate with you.'

'Felipe will, of course. But when last seen, Rita was stomping off in a tantrum.'

'What on earth for?' she asked, imagining that Rita would be an accomplished tantrum-thrower.

'She and I had words, you might say, over the little tale she told you about my wanting you to leave the station.'

'But why should that cause trouble between you—it was true!'

'Yes, it was true, all right. At least the part about my wanting you to go was. The reasons she gave were not.'

'Adam, none of this makes sense ... I'm completely bewildered!'

'I'm not surprised. It took me quite a while to figure out what was going on myself.'

Jensa twisted to face him squarely. 'Let me get this straight—Rita said that you were angry over the accident.'

'I was. Furious.'

'And about my work, she——' Jensa stopped short. She had no desire to accuse another woman of lying. She was beginning to regret the entire conversation.

'It's not in the Miss Welles code to squeal on her, is it?' he said gently. 'So I'll do it for you. She probably said all kinds of unpleasant things about how I felt about you and your work.'

'I don't think I want to talk any more about Rita.

What she did or did not say doesn't matter. The point is, you wanted me gone. Now please—can't we just drop it?'

'No, Jensa, we can't.'

She felt his hands come to rest on her shoulders, then move caressingly down her arms. He bent as if to place his parted lips on hers, and she panicked. She could not endure that kind of emotional and physical torment again. She would simply fall apart.

She bolted from the sofa and stood before the windows drawing ragged breaths. 'I told you,' she said, forming each word with care, 'that I didn't want you to do that to me ever again!'

'All right, then,' he replied quietly. 'I'll finish what I started to say. The reason I wanted you to go was that your near-death scared the hell out of me. And made me face the fact that I'm in love with you.'

The room, the entire city spread out before her, simply disappeared. She saw nothing any longer. She could only hear his words ringing over and over in her ears.

His voice grew harsh. 'Do you understand what I'm saying, Jensa? I knew that unless you went—immediately—my resistance would crumble altogether. So I put on one last front of coldness. I know it was cruel and perverse, but I hurt you because I loved you so much. You were such a threat, you see, to the defences I'd built so carefully against real love and intimacy.'

Slowly she turned to face him. She searched his face for that trace of cruelty, that cynicism that had marked it since their first encounter, and found none. She saw only openness and intensity that moved her in a way she had never experienced before.

'But I did leave—you got what you wanted, Adam,'

she cried in a tremulous voice. 'Why come here now and start all this up again?'

'Because it was no good any more. Even my last refuge, my work, could never be the same after sharing it with you. We were so right together, you and I—I couldn't conceive of going on with it without you. So I paced the floor endlessly and debated and raged until I finally drove poor Maria crazy. She had quite a few choice words for me, I can tell you. About the way I'd treated you. About what Rita had said to you. And she told me something else, Jensa. That you didn't despise me for the way I treated you.'

He looked at her expectantly. Slowly, tentatively, he reached out for her again, and this time she did not resist. 'I love you, Adam. I love you so very much,' she whispered as he pressed her to him. He kissed her then in that way that brought her breath in short, exquisite gasps.

She laid her head against his broad chest, weak with the wonder and longing that were washing over her. 'There's so much I don't understand,' she said. 'I was so sure you felt only contempt for me as a woman.'

Adam led her to the sofa and enfolded her in his arms. 'When I first laid eyes on you in Puerto Madryn— before I even knew who you were—I found you maddeningly attractive. Later, watching you work, I knew that you were also gifted and brilliant. But it was the morning after the calf died that I began to understand the depth of my feeling for you. I'd watched you work till your hands bled, for a dying animal. I'd watched you cry for it—not out of maudlin sentimentality, but because you felt a kinship with another intelligence. I knew then that you were the one woman who could share my world with me. It was then that I started to fight my love for you like a crazy man.'

'I remember,' she said softly. 'I was so confused after Muffin died. I thought we'd finally broken through our animosity, were friends, at least. But you became more hostile than ever.'

He held her tightly to him. 'Can you forgive me for that, Jensa? I told myself to reduce it all to physical passion. I'd see the hurt in your eyes and it would tear me apart, darling!'

She laid two delicate fingertips against the strongly carved mouth. 'Hush,' she said, smiling at him with great tenderness, 'you mustn't torture yourself with that—it's over. Promise me you won't.'

'I will ... if you'll promise to marry me as soon as it's humanly possible!'

She looked at him and dimpled with delight. 'I think you're serious, Dr Ryder!'

'Of course I am. We'll fly to Montreal tonight and we can be married there. Josh can stand up for us—he was probably plotting this all along, the old fox!'

'And just where are we to begin our marital bliss, if I might ask one tiny, practical question?'

He looked properly thoughtful. 'We could live somewhere civilised—I may *look* like a disreputable ne'er-do-well most of the time, but I'm not without means. My father inherited money—a great deal, really—and like me, he didn't squander it. So it all came down to me. I confess that I enjoy coming up for a breather in the civilised world every now and then. So you see, we could settle down and live a life of idle luxury somewhere if you'd like——'

'I know,' she said, her eyes sparkling, 'we could—but we won't, will we? Neither one of us would be happy with such an existence. In fact, I strongly suspect you have plans brewing already, Dr Ryder!'

'Guilty,' he said cheerfully. 'How does a year in the Indian Ocean sound to you? And a honeymoon on a rocking old tub of a research vessel? In between tests and kisses, I thought we might turn out a couple of books together. There's a study I've been dying to do on an Indian dolphin.'

Jensa laughed and looked at him with eyes shining with love. 'Oddly enough, Doctor, it sounds very good —I must be as mad as you are!'

But a tiny frown line appeared on her brow and she bent her head and toyed with the leather button on his jacket. She found herself suddenly shy, a fact she thought remarkable, given the intimacy of their last embrace.

'What is it?' he demanded sternly, tilting her chin up to him with one finger. 'It's no use trying to hide your feelings from me, you know.'

'I was thinking ... I don't know why ... about babies.'

'What about them?' he asked gently.

'Well ... I want them, that's all. And my work. I've always assumed that, with the right man, I'd have them both.'

'You do, I believe, have the right man. So why the frown?'

'I was trying to picture babies on research vessels and out-of-the-way laboratories,' she replied glumly.

'I think it makes an altogether charming picture myself,' he replied easily. 'I think a child would be lucky to have the entire world for a nursery. And with you as a mother, it would feel well anchored in life no matter how much roaming we do. You and I are quite capable of teaching the A.B.C., my dear. And when the time comes, we can always spend the school year in some university town teaching and working on books while the little Ryders try to gobble down some dry old book-learning!'

She looked at him feeling wonder at his infectious enthusiasm for life. Nothing seemed impossible with such a man!

'No more problems?' he asked, holding her at arm's length.

'No more problems,' she replied.

He brought her to him once again. There was silence in the room for long moments after that. Finally, as Adam withdrew his lips from a hungry caress of her neck, he whispered, 'You and I must go and do that sightseeing. A hotel room is decidedly not the place where we should be right now! Our time will come—and soon, my darling.'

Yes, she thought, looking up at him in wonder and in joy. She knew now that neither her heart nor her body had betrayed her, after all, in urging her to love this man. With him, she would be safe and cherished, always.

ROMANCE

Variety is the spice of romance

Each month, Mills & Boon publish new romances. New stories about people falling in love. A world of variety in romance – from the best writers in the romantic world. Choose from these titles in March.

LORD OF THE LAND Margaret Rome
CALL UP THE STORM Jane Donnelly
BETRAYAL Charlotte Lamb
THE DEVIL'S ADVOCATE Vanessa James
VISION OF LOVE Elizabeth Graham
CHAINS OF GOLD Yvonne Whittal
CLOUDED RAPTURE Margaret Pargeter
THE FLAWED MARRIAGE Penny Jordan
MIDSUMMER STAR Betty Neels
LOVE'S ONLY DECEPTION Carole Mortimer
PASSIONATE ENEMIES Kathryn Cranmer
SEA LIGHTNING Linda Harrel

On sale where you buy paperbacks. If you require further information or have any difficulty obtaining them, write to: Mills & Boon Reader Service, PO Box 236, Thornton Road, Croydon, Surrey CR9 3RU, England.

Mills & Boon
the rose of romance

FREE-an exclusive Anne Mather title, MELTING FIRE

At Mills & Boon we value very highly the opinion of our readers. What <u>you</u> tell us about what you like in romantic reading is important to us.

So if you will tell us which Mills & Boon romance you have most enjoyed reading lately, we will send you a copy of MELTING FIRE by Anne Mather – absolutely FREE.

There are no snags, no hidden charges. It's absolutely FREE.

Just send us your answer to our question, and help us to bring you the best in romantic reading.

CLAIM YOUR FREE BOOK NOW

Simply fill in details below, cut out and post to: Mills & Boon Reader Service, FREEPOST, P.O. Box 236, Croydon, Surrey CR9 9EL.

The Mills & Boon story I have most enjoyed during the past 6 months is:

TITLE _____

AUTHOR_____   BLOCK LETTERS, PLEASE

NAME (Mrs/Miss) _____   EP4

ADDRESS _____

_____ POST CODE _____

Offer restricted to ONE Free Book a year per household. Applies only in U.K. and Eire. CUT OUT AND POST TODAY – NO STAMP NEEDED.

Mills & Boon
the rose of romance